TANGLED IN TIME

BOOK TWO

The Burning Queen

Other Books by Kathryn Lasky

Kathryn Lasky

BOOK TWO

The Burning Queen

HARPER
An Imprint of HarperCollinsPublishers

ISBN 978-0-06-269328-0

Typography by
19 20 21 22 23   CPIG   10 9 8 7 6 5 4 3 2 1

First Edition

For Luella Grace Knight,
a passionate reader

Contents

Torn

Ominous Signs

The Burning Queen

TANGLED IN TIME

BOOK TWO

The Burning Queen

THE INDIANAPOLIS TRIBUNE

Bow Ties Not Just for Guys?

by Betsy Langford

Fashion blogger and Lincoln Middle School student Rose Ashley and a group of her friends have started a new trend—bow ties.

"Bow ties are gender free," says Rose. "They add a lot to an outfit and can help express your personality." Before moving to Indianapolis, when she was a fifth grader in Philadelphia, Rose started a bow tie of the month club. "Bow ties are really easy to make. So I just posted the directions on my blog and picked out an easy-to-find fabric, and kids would copy them." Now, however, she and her team of "Christmas Elves," as she calls them, are making and selling the bow ties. All proceeds go to the Indy Christmas Fund for Needy Children. So far they have raised almost $1,000. Members of her team are fellow Lincoln Middle School students Susan Gold, Sibby Huang, Anand Preet, Myles Randolph, Kevin

Ellsworth, Joe Mallory, and Sayid Nassim.

"We use all kinds of fabric and styles," Susan Gold explains.

"There are many kinds of styles," Rose interjects. "My personal favorite is the James Bond style. Nobody wore it better than Sean Connery in *Goldfinger*." What about *Skyfall* with Daniel Craig? this reporter asked. "Okay, but he doesn't have the chops to really carry it off. Sorry, Daniel."

Susan Gold is sporting a bright green tie that suddenly flashes red. "LED light. I sewed it in." She giggles. "I don't think Rose approves. She's somewhat of a purist."

"Not really," Rose protests. "Bow ties have evolved like everything else."

It turns out that Rose Ashley is a bit of a fashion historian. "You know, the first bow ties date back to the seventeenth century during the Thirty Years' War in Europe. Croatian mercenaries would use scarves to hold together the openings of their shirts at the neck."

Well, hats off and bow ties on to these Indianapolis middle graders for their energy and generosity in helping to make a better Christmas for many children in need.

Torn

Chapter 1

Fingers Crossed

"*Never . . . never . . . never!*" *Rose muttered in her head. Her* fingers were crossed and still jammed in her pockets, but the pockets were different—not the deep ones of her kirtle but tight shallow jeans pockets. The floor was hard beneath her knees—not wood, but stone or cement. And the scent. Fresher. And yet she still had her eyes clamped shut. She was almost afraid to open them. The last thing she had been aware of was a slight smell. Yes, Queen Mary, who now wanted to enslave her, did have a little body odor problem. Why didn't they have real deodorant in the sixteenth century, instead of those stupid little cloth bags filled with dried flower petals?

But the scent that swirled about Rose now was not of

dried flowers but fresh, just-blossoming flowers. A sweet, alluring fragrance suffused the air. Slowly Rose opened her eyes. She looked up. A fifteen-foot vine with beautiful pink blooms fell through the darkness. The vines could have been fireworks mutely exploding in the night. But they weren't. They were hibiscus, and they were cascading from the central cupola of the greenhouse. She was back! Back in her grandmother Rosalinda's greenhouse. Back in Indianapolis, Indiana. Back in what she now called her home century.

But was she *safe*? She uncrossed her fingers. She looked around. The words of the nasty queen, Mary Tudor, still rang in her ears. *Rose Ashley, we hear you are excellent in the wardrobe, have a way with a needle, and can do fine and delicate work. You shall from here on be our mistress of the wardrobe. . . . You shall serve me, queen of this realm, and swear loyalty to me above all others save God. Do you swear? Down on your knees and swear.* That was when Rose had crossed her fingers and lied to this new queen.

Rose had previously served Princess Elizabeth, who, although very demanding and imperious, was not the nasty piece of work that Queen Mary was. However, when their half brother, King Edward—barely fifteen—had died, Mary had ascended the throne, to everyone's horror.

That was the bad news. Not just for Rose, who would have to serve this vile piece of royal nastiness. But also bad news for Princess Elizabeth. Mary liked to take things that belonged to Elizabeth. She was insanely jealous of her half sister—of her youth, for one thing, since Queen Mary was seventeen years older. But she was also envious of Elizabeth's beauty and her smarts. Elizabeth was the smartest kid Rose had ever met. She was insanely smart—spoke French, Italian, Latin—yes, she actually spoke Latin! If she had lived in the twenty-first century and been in Rose's school, she could have been a mathlete and gone to the state championship.

Elizabeth was already doing trigonometry when she was just eleven years old. In Rose's home century, you didn't do that until high school. When Rose had once asked Elizabeth if she knew calculus, the princess's face turned blank. And when she asked Rose to explain what calculus was, Rose's mind turned blank. She almost blurted out, "How should I know? That's not until high school." But she stopped herself in the nick of time. As soon as she got back to her home century, she googled calculus and found out it hadn't been discovered until the seventeenth century! By Isaac Newton, no less.

Well, no matter how you looked at it, Queen Mary was definitely bad news. This was in fact a typical bad news/good news situation. The good news—Rose was back. The bad news was that her father, Nicholas Oliver, was not with her, nor was her sixteenth-century best friend, Franny. Then, just as she was reflecting on all this, she felt something brush against her leg. Good news! September! She gasped and reached for the bright orange cat. Picking her up, she pressed her to her chest. The cat wiggled and began head-butting Rose. Head-butting was the supreme expression of affection for cats. Sometimes September did not return with Rose to their home century but lingered in the sixteenth instead. Better mousing back then, due to lousy housekeeping habits. All the palaces had stables chock-full of mice and other less charming rodents.

As she walked upstairs to her bedroom, Rose felt the sudden vibration of her cell phone in the other pocket of her jeans. She took it out and looked at it. The time was 8:45 p.m. and it was Susan calling, of course. Susan Gold was Rose's best friend in her home century.

"Hey, Rose, what's up?" Susan said cheerfully.

Rose was always a bit disoriented when she first returned to the present day. "Uh . . ." She couldn't answer immediately.

"Whatcha been up to?"

"Uh . . . French homework." A sort-of lie. She had been doing it before she'd left. But the fact was, none of her friends knew about this. This . . . was there any other word for it? Rose had a definitely weird skill, this *ability* of hers. She could travel through time. Was it a skill or her fate? Rose often wondered.

"I thought you'd be sewing with all those new bow tie orders. Not to mention the costumes for the Snow Show."

Rose glanced over at the costumes piled on a futon in the corner of her bedroom. They were awaiting their final touches, which meant glitter and glitz. Skaters loved the glitz—sequins, feathers, whatever. The costumes were designed to dazzle AND accentuate the skater's motion. A jump was all the more beautiful with a fringe of glittery spangles sewn to the hem of a skating skirt. Fake feathers attached to sleeves suggested flight. Seams were often accentuated with rhinestones. To study up on all this, the Indianapolis Skating Club had given her tickets for her and two friends (Joe and Susan) to see the *Disney on Ice* show. They even got to go backstage and look at the costumes. The wardrobe mistress gave a few old ones to Rose so she could study them. Apparently a single costume only lasted for a couple of weeks during show season.

"The costumes are almost done," Rose said. "Just have to sew on some fringe and stuff. Then I'll get to work on this last order of bow ties." She yawned.

"You sound tired, Rose."

"Hmmm . . ." She was about to say that you would be too if you'd traveled back five centuries and watched a prince die and a complete rat get the crown, and then were made to get down on your knees and swear to serve that rat queen. Not to mention—Dad! *I miss my dad.* Tears started to run down her face. She couldn't cry on the phone with Susan. There was no way she could explain it all to her.

"Listen, I have to go. This French is hard. I don't really get the difference between the *passé composé* and *passé antérieur*." Rose sighed.

"Oh, one is really for speaking, like 'We went to the Louvre.' *Nous sommes allées au Louvre*. The other is *nous eûmes au Louvre*, and that's just for literary use, you know, in books. The first one is kind of regular time. The second is when you're in a literary time zone."

"Oh," Rose said. That was, of course, her problem. She seemed to slip between time, between tenses and time zones. There wasn't exactly "regular time" for Rose.

"Get it?" Susan asked.

"Sort of," Rose replied.

"The Mean Queens have been back for two weeks now. It seems like forever, doesn't it?" Susan said. Rose caught her breath. Susan wasn't talking about Mary Tudor, Queen of England. She was talking about Carrie, Brianna, and Lisa—also known as the Trio of Doom. The Nemeses on the Premises. They had all three been suspended from school for two days after playing a terrible trick on Joe, Susan's sort-of boyfriend. They basically sabotaged his skates, so that he fell and broke his ankle. Meaning he was out of the Snow Show. But Brianna was out too—not only out of school for two days, but also banished from the Indianapolis Skating Club for good. Served her right. Sometimes Rose felt as if she were caught not just between two centuries, but between two sets of Mean Queens as well.

Well, Princess Elizabeth was not a queen, of course, but she could be mean too. Not as mean as Mary, but kind of spiteful. Like the time she took Rose's locket. The locket that her father had made. The rose-shaped locket that had the photo of her and her mom in it . . . and that of her dad, Nicholas Oliver, the goldsmith to the court! It was downright mean that Elizabeth had snatched that locket from her, with the lame excuse that only royals could wear the Tudor Rose. Rose crossed her fingers again and sent up a little prayer.

Oh please, don't let Princess Elizabeth figure out the secret to open-ing that locket!

Chapter 2

Fish Sticks and Other Lunchroom Atrocities

"*G*ood *morning, students!*" It was the voice of Ms. Fuentes, the principal of Lincoln Middle School. "'Tis the season to be merry, but also grateful. And we are grateful to the Bow Tie Team—Susan Gold, Rose Ashley, Joe Mallory, Anand Preet, Sibby Huang, Kevin Ellsworth, Sayid Nassim, and Myles Randolph—for their extraordinary efforts in raising money for Indianapolis's most needy children. They have all been awarded certificates of community service from the *Indianapolis Tribune*. They will be presented today at morning assembly."

"Myles." Carrie's snarky voice slithered through the air. "Your hands can barely move. How can you sew? All you can do is push the button for your wheelchair with one finger."

Rose turned around in her desk. "Myles happens to be our chief financial officer, Carrie. He does all the math and bookkeeping for this project."

"Please! No talking, young ladies," ordered Mr. Ross, the homeroom and language arts teacher. Rose felt her skin prickle. She hated it when Mr. Ross called them "young ladies." Did he think he was making them feel grown up? He wasn't. Rose had always felt that there was something belittling about addressing middle school girls as "young ladies." There was certainly nothing ladylike in Carrie's remarks. It was pure bully.

Myles shot her a glance from his wheelchair. Even though he could only move one hand because of his cerebral palsy, his eyes said it all. "Let it go, Rose."

The irony of Mr. Ross calling them "young ladies" hit her squarely as she looked at the words of the week on the greenboard. In five minutes Mr. Ross would erase the words on the board and then they would begin their spelling review. The students would be required to write out each word after Mr. Ross said it, then write it in a sentence. The words for this week were: chimera, egotistical, superior, condescend, betray, maniacal, belligerent, lackadaisical, and . . . ta-da! PATRONIZING. That was exactly the definition of calling a seventh-grade girl "young lady."

Quiet descended on the homeroom as Mr. Ross said the words and the students wrote them down. Mr. Ross was very pale with red-rimmed eyes, and he kept a huge box of tissues on his desk. It seemed to Rose as if he were always on the brink of a sneeze. He appeared hyperallergic to something. After the class had written down all the words, they spent the next twenty minutes writing sentences. You got double points if you could use more than a single word within one sentence. Rose felt her brain rev up as she began to write the last sentence.

To address seventh-grade girls as "young ladies" is not simply condescending but in truth patronizing, and although it might suggest apparent kindness, it actually betrays the sense of superiority of the speaker.

There! thought Rose. She ground in her pencil tip for the period at the end of her triple-whammy sentence.

When they finished the spelling review, Mr. Ross collected the papers.

"Now please take out *To Kill a Mockingbird* and we'll discuss the first chapter."

He turned his back and used his laptop to project a sentence from the book on the screen.

Maycomb was an old town, but it was a tired old town when I first knew it. In rainy weather the streets turned to red slop.... Somehow, it was hotter then ... bony mules hitched to Hoover carts flicked flies in the sweltering shade of the live oaks on the square.

"This, ladies and gents, is PERSONIFICATION!" He shouted the word as if he had invented it. *Jeez,* thought Rose, *what a way to ruin a wonderful book.* Rose must have made a face, for she'd caught Mr. Ross's eye.

"Do you have something to say, Rose?"

"No, no . . . just a random thought."

"Oh, please share it."

"No, I'd rather not." *Mr. Ross does not like me.*

Susan's hand shot up. "I think it's interesting to note that Harper Lee spent more time in New York City that she did in Monroeville, Alabama. Because she became so famous, she liked the anonymity of a big city."

"Well, yes, Susan, that is interesting, but I was going to ask if any of you understood what I mean by personification?"

"Uh . . . ," Susan said. "I think it's describing something in a human way that is not human—like the town of Maycomb."

"She wanted to get out of Maycomb and go to New York 'cause it was just too boring," Tom, the boy who sat behind Susan, offered. "I know about small, boring towns. I lived in Kokomo until last year—really boring. Indianapolis is like New York compared to Kokomo."

"Whhhaaaat?! Are you kidding?" said Joe.

A boisterous argument broke out. Mr. Ross flushed, the

way he always did when he lost control of his class. Someone made a fart noise in the back of the room. Or maybe it was a real fart.

"Ladies and gentlemen. Ladies . . . ."

Oh, just shut up! thought Rose. But she saw the look of near panic in Mr. Ross's eyes and almost felt sorry for him.

Almost but not quite. . . .

Rose was sitting at lunch at her usual table with Susan and Joe, Anand, Kevin, and Myles.

Rose cast a glance over at Joe's plate.

"Barfaroni," Joe said. "But better than fish sticks in a taco with cheese on top . . . I just couldn't." He paused and looked at Marisol, a new girl who was making her way toward their table. But then, within another second, she tripped. Her tray went flying. Her own barfaroni splattered on a sixth grader's sweater. The sixth grader, Jenny, began wailing and jumped up from her chair.

"My grandma gave me this sweater. It's cashmere. You . . . you . . . clumsy girl. You've ruined my heirloom sweater!"

"Heirloom," Susan muttered. "Give me a break."

"Stupido!" Jenny shouted.

Marisol turned pale. Her eyes darted around the room like a trapped animal looking for escape.

"I can't believe she just said that!" Rose gasped.

"Look at them! Look at the Trio of Doom." Joe leaned over and whispered to Rose. "They're trying not to laugh."

"Duet of Doom. No Brianna," Rose said.

Indeed, Carrie's and Lisa's mouths were locked between smirks and howls of merriment. Meanwhile Jenny was giving an Academy Award–winning performance of outrage. "Do you know how much this cost? This sweater?"

Anand, who was sitting next to Joe, jumped up to help Marisol salvage what she could from her lunch. She had arrived only a few weeks ago. Rose scooted over and made room for Marisol. "Don't listen to them, Marisol. They're just a bunch of jerks."

"Hey! Look over there—seismic shift," Kevin said suddenly.

"What are you talking about?" Rose asked.

"Okay, don't be obvious, but look who's sitting in the corner—alone."

They all slid their eyes around to steal a glance.

"Brianna alone?" Joe said. "Impossible."

"Then it *is* a duet," Myles said. It was difficult for him to turn around in his wheelchair.

"Who will replace her?" Anand asked.

"Someone, I'm sure," Rose said. "Power vacuum."

"Power?" Marisol whispered. She appeared frightened. Very frightened.

"Oh, don't worry, it's just an expression," Rose said.

"A law of physics, actually," Anand said. "Any space in which the pressure is lower than the atmospheric pressure. I'll demonstrate." He began sucking on his straw. The liquid rose in the straw. "See?" he said, looking up at Marisol. "I reduced the pressure by sucking and the milk flowed up. Same thing over there." He tipped his head toward Carrie and Lisa, who were sitting at a table with a couple of sixth graders. "One of those kids will fill in for Brianna."

"I'd put my money on the cashmere sweater heiress, Jenny," Rose replied in a scalding voice.

Jenny was quite tiny, more the size of a fourth grader than a sixth grader, and right now she was looking up at Carrie with adoring eyes. Was she seeking approval? Jenny's once almost white-blond hair now shimmered pink and had a spritz of glitter as well.

"What's with the pink hair?" Joe asked.

"Well, look at Carrie with her blue streak. Obviously, she is worshipping at the altar of the Mean Queens—the glitter like Lisa, and the pink hair. What more do you need to know?"

"Looks like a wad of bubble gum," Rose muttered.

Jenny had a tiny turned-up nose and she very much reminded Rose of Tinker Bell since she wore her hair in a little knot on top of her head. Her bangs fell in a slant across her forehead. It was the exact same hairstyle as Tinker Bell had in the Disney movie. *Perky!* Rose thought. *Perky with a capital P!* There was a rumor that Jenny's mom was grooming her for the tryouts for the next season of *America's Next Top Tween Model*.

"Hey, Rose," Myles said. "Look over there; Mr. Ross is trying to get your attention."

Rose looked up and saw Mr. Ross waving at her.

Uh...oh..., thought Rose, and got up from her seat and walked over to him.

"I didn't mean to interrupt your lunch, Rose."

"No, it's okay. I was done." *Lie.*

"Well, I'd rather discuss this in homeroom."

"Fine."

When they got to the homeroom, Mr. Ross pulled out the spelling papers. "I want to apologize."

"For what?" she asked, and dipped her head. She could not face those watery translucent eyes that looked as if they were on the edge of tears. She heard him sniffle.

"For this." He slid a paper toward her.

Her own handwriting glared back at her. *To address seventh-grade girls as "young ladies" is not simply condescending, but in truth patronizing, and although it might suggest apparent kindness, it actually betrays the sense of superiority of the speaker.*

"There is so much truth to what you say. As Harper Lee says in *To Kill A Mockingbird*, 'You never really understand a person until you consider things from his point of view . . . until you climb into his skin and walk around in it.'" He gave a little chuckle, and this was followed by a gigantic sneeze. "Sorry about that. I'm allergic to a lot of stuff, especially this season—holly, certain kinds of Christmas trees . . ."

"Cats?"

"Yes, some cats. But the point is, Rose, that I never considered how the term might sound condescending, and patronizing. . . . I failed to climb into a seventh grader's skin and walk around in it."

"It's okay," Rose muttered, and then paused.

"It's not okay," he said. Rose wanted to try to tell him that it would be impossible for him to climb into her skin and walk around . . . walk between two centuries. "Well, I'm sorry." He picked up a red pencil and marked the paper A++.

Chapter 3

Know
Thine Enemy

"*Do you ever wonder about Marisol?*" *Rose asked Susan as they* picked over some shoes in their favorite vintage store, Old Souls.

"What do you mean?"

"Well, you know, she just showed up a few weeks ago, kind of mysteriously. And she seems . . . I don't know, kind of scared of something."

"I think she's pretty smart, because her English has really improved fast," Susan said. "She's in that English as a second language program, isn't she?"

"I think so," Rose replied.

"But I don't know why you think she's scared of something. I just think she looks tired a lot," Susan said.

"You do?"

"Yeah, in math—and she's pretty good in math—I guess that's why she's in our class. Math being a kind of universal language." Susan picked up a strange-looking coat. "What the heck is this?"

"Ahh . . ." A voice tinkled from the other side of the rack. A little lady with a tumble of curls piled atop her head toddled out. "I wondered how long it would take you to discover that. It's a pelisse. Quite the fashion about two hundred years ago. Once fur trimmed. The embroidery work is gorgeous. I'll sell it to you cheap, because moths have feasted on most of it."

"But not the sleeves," Rose said.

"But what are you going to do with just sleeves?" Susan asked.

"Turn them into pants—cropped pants. Look, it's velvet and the embroidery is beautiful."

"Oh yes, in the mid-1800s there was quite a passion for floral embroidery on coats and jackets," said the little lady, Elsie, the proprietor of the store.

The flowers reminded Rose of the long dangling vines of pink blossoms that hung in the greenhouse. Their scent had greeted her return from sixteenth-century England and Greenwich Palace. Rose wondered if her father was at Greenwich now. Or was he back in Stoke-on-the-Wold, sitting at his bench, forging and hammering gold into beautiful pieces for this new queen. For he was a goldsmith to the court, an important position, especially now.

Rose bit her lip lightly, as she often did when thinking. It was all so unfair. Her father was there. She was here. Should she even risk going back, back to serve that horrible queen? But wouldn't it be worth it if she could meet up with her dad and somehow, some way, get him to her century? Her home century. She knew it wasn't his, but he would adjust.

"Would you take fifteen dollars for this, Elsie?"

Elsie looked at Rose. Her blue eyes that normally radiated cheer suddenly seemed to dim. It was as if an eclipse were occurring. A cloud cover of pity?

"Oh, that would be too much. You can have it for ten," she replied gaily. Although to Rose it sounded a bit forced. *Do I have "orphan" written all over me?* Rose wondered.

As they left the store, Rose could almost feel Elsie's eyes on her back. *She's wondering about me. But there's no way she would know.* Rose pushed the feeling from herself and instead began to think about Marisol. Why did this girl, with her liquid brown eyes, intrigue her? She seemed very fragile yet strong. Strong in ways that Rose couldn't quite imagine.

But it was the questions not about Marisol but her own predicament that continued to haunt Rose. Would it be too risky to go back?

An hour later Rose was in the greenhouse with her grandmother. They often ate their dinner at one end of the seedling table.

"You're fiddling with your food, child," her grandmother said. "Something bothering you?"

"Uh . . . no, not really . . ." Her gran knew about her travels through time. Rosalinda Ashley was in fact a traveler herself. As Rose's mother had been. "We have the gene," her grandmother had said. But those times when her gran had traversed centuries were not as dangerous as the time that Rose would be facing if she returned. Mary Tudor would be known as Bloody Mary within a few years, for her determination to burn heretics—Protestants and others who would not follow the Catholic Church—at the stake. How many would she kill?

"Know thine enemy," Gran muttered.

Rose stiffened. It was as if her gran were reading her mind. Creepy! "What?" Rose exclaimed. Her grandmother was bending over a tray of seedlings she had just started a week before. "Mite blight. Get the spray gun."

Rose brought it over, and Rosalinda began squirting the seedlings. Her jaw was set and her eyes narrowed behind the thick lenses of her glasses. "The little devils. This is it! I shall eradicate them!" her grandmother croaked as she squeezed the trigger on the spray bottle.

Gran certainly knew her enemy, but did Rose know

hers—Queen Mary? When the seedlings' enemy was vanquished, her grandmother gave a big yawn and dropped her head to her chest. She would be asleep in another minute. Betty, her gran's caretaker, came into the greenhouse.

"Asleep?" she whispered.

"Not yet!" Rosalinda snapped. "Why would I be asleep in the thick of battle?"

"I think the battle's over, Gran. You got every one of those mites."

"How would you know?" Her gran looked up at her blankly. There were often these moments when her grandmother simply did not recognize her own granddaughter. They were brief but rather unnerving for Rose. She didn't resent these lapses, but they just made her feel so utterly alone.

Rose, after all, was a sort-of orphan. Her mother had been killed in a fiery car crash. So Rose had come to live with her gran just a few months before. Her grandmother, Rosalinda Ashley, had been her only living relative until she discovered her father in that other century. She had never suspected she even had a father—though of course she knew that somewhere there was one—but then she had discovered the beautiful rose pendant with its secret pin. It was Franny, her friend from that distant century, who had found the pendant first. She discovered the pin in the locket, and in opening it saw the pictures. The images seemed very strange to Franny, for she had never seen a photograph, of course. Photography would not be invented for another several centuries. It was a photo of Rose's mom and Rose, looking very twenty-first-century in their bathing suits, posing on a beach in Florida. In the photo, Rose was about five years old and wearing her Little Mermaid bathing suit and her swim goggles hanging from her neck with cartoon frog eyes on top. She clutched a Mickey Mouse pocketbook. At that age she seldom went far without her Disney gear. In the other half of the locket was a picture of a man. Not a modern-day man, but definitely one from the sixteenth century, with a trim beard and a high ruff, the fashion of the time.

That man, Rose learned, was in fact her father—Nicholas Oliver, goldsmith for the royal court. He had made that locket. Rose had only met him twice in the sixteenth century. But now she was determined to bring him back into her century, her home century, the twenty-first. She'd bring Franny back too if that were possible. Franny, a scullery girl in Hatfield House, was her best friend in that century. Susan was her best in this one. But she doubted that Franny would leave, as she had a family there. Rose had discovered that Franny and her mom and dad were also time travelers. But the distance they had come was not so far in time, just close to a hundred and fifty years, from 1692 America to the mid-1500s England. They had fled the witch hangings in Salem,

Massachusetts, where Franny's mother had been condemned to die. But now Queen Mary was burning Protestants in the very land where her family had sought refuge. Burnings, hangings, what would be next? Boiling in oil? Oh, the sixteenth-century mind was so creative in devising ways to kill people.

Then it struck Rose—Franny was truly in danger! Yet again. For Franny would no more become a Catholic than sprout wings and fly. She was a very good and observant Protestant. If you asked her what her religion was, she would say C of E. The Church of England that had been established, and headed, by King Henry VIII. But now there was this new, or rather old, church headed by the pope in Rome, and not the king or queen of England. Franny would hate that. She and her family might have to flee again.

And how bad was it in England? When Rose was last there, the young king had just died. Mary had not even been queen for a full day yet when she had ordered Rose to swear allegiance. The burnings hadn't started, but they might begin soon—perhaps right after the coronation. Her gran's voice rolled through her mind. *Know thine enemy.*

Okay, she decided. *Forget the French homework.* She'd finished the costume for the Snow Show—the dragon for St. George—sewing the last scales on the armature that Michael Huang would wear. Michael had taken over the role from Joe after Joe had broken his ankle. What she had to do now was study not French, but history—and not Indiana history, which seemed to be the single focus in school this year. She was supposed to do a report on the smallpox epidemic of 1752 that had nearly wiped out the Native American population. Oh, imagine if Queen Mary had caught smallpox! How many lives would have been saved?

Chapter 4

A Creak on the Staircase

Rose went up to her room. She found September plopped on her desk. Plopped on top of her laptop, the cat's favorite spot, as it radiated a nice bit of heat. Luckily Rose had a separate monitor. A huge one. Must have cost her gran a thousand dollars. Right now there were cat videos playing. One of September's favorites: a cat trying to climb into a boot. Then Rose's favorite—a cat emerging from the cushions of a deep sofa. First only its pink little nose was visible, poking out from between the two big puffy cushions. Then the tip of its tail slipped out from behind a back cushion. From Rose's perspective, it was as if a cat were in the process of being assembled in some sort of random fashion. September always gave a happy little squeak when the whole cat was revealed.

"Okay, September. No more screen time."

She turned and gave Rose a withering look. A how-could-you? look. A very-adolescent-girl-feline look. In fact, Rose thought, it was slightly *patronizing*, not to put too fine a point on it. She shoved September off her desk and put her iPad on the floor. "You can play cat games with my iPad." Again September gave her a withering gaze, arched her back, and walked stiffly away. Rose sighed and turned toward the computer. September was a lot about show. She had to show her disdain first, and then within a couple of minutes she'd be back. A real drama queen! Better than a mean queen. Rose leaned down and hit the start button for the cat fishing game. There was the sound of bubbles bursting softly. September came back. Within seconds she started to play, her paws flashing as she batted the swimming fish on the screen. Within fifteen seconds September had advanced to Master Level.

Rose suddenly realized that before she could get to studying history, she had a report to finish up for science class. She had decided to write about leprosy. That was sort of historical. She definitely could kill two birds with one stone—leprosy! She'd seen a few lepers when she was back in the sixteenth century. That's what had gotten Rose interested in doing a report on it for science. Lepers were treated like criminals—rounded up and sent off to special leprosy hospitals that were more like prisons. If there was no nearby hospital, they were forced to wear bells around their necks to warn people they were coming. She remembered once walking with the other wardrobe maid, Sara, in the village near Hampton Court Palace. She first heard a bell and then saw a decrepit figure coming round a bend. Sara screeched and grabbed her hand, pulling Rose into a ditch on the far side of the road. "Wrap your apron around your mouth. Try not to breathe! Leper coming our way!" That was the first time Rose had heard of leprosy. Sara later gave a vivid description about how the disease ate away at one's flesh and then at one's fingers and toes, which eventually started to drop off. Ms. Lafferty, their science teacher, wanted them to do reports on various medical conditions and diseases—those spread by contagion, those that were inherited, and those that were congenital or caused by birth trauma.

Ms. Lafferty thought leprosy was a great idea for a report, but when Rose told her that she was going to title the report "For Whom the Bell Tolls," she said that wasn't a good idea. There was already a novel by the same name, from one of America's greatest writers, Ernest Hemingway. So now Rose had to think of a new title . . . but first she had to finish the report.

With September finally settled down, Rose could concentrate. She put in her earbuds. No way could she think about leprosy and the strange sick world of Mary Tudor without some cool music. BWB was her favorite band these days.

BWB stood for Boyz Will Be Boyz. And her and Susan's favorite singer was Yuu Park, a Korean kid who was *soooooooo* cute.

Her favorite song started softly in her ears. It was a sound made just for her, and Park's voice was perfect. He was whispering it to her, right in her ear. She was sure.

I'm in between
In some lost and found
But really lost and never found
No one cares I have no place
Is this my fault or is there no race
No place no race just give me grace
La na la na la la na na

Those nonsense syllables whispered softly in Rose's ear and soothed her as she googled Queen Mary Tudor. She and leprosy coexisted in the same era, two bad diseases. Mary became queen July 6, 1553, the day her half brother, King Edward, died. It would be three more months until her coronation. But she was still queen. She could do a lot of damage before that crown actually sat on her head. Rose continued googling.

"Good Lord," she muttered. "Who's this?" A picture popped up, a young woman, one Lady Jane Grey, who . . . Hope sprang in Rose's heart. "She claimed the throne for nine days!" Rose opened her eyes wide. She remembered the young king talking to her about Lady Jane Grey. He wanted her to succeed him instead of Mary. Well, apparently she had, but only for nine days before she was hauled off to prison. Jane was held as a prisoner at the Tower and was convicted of high treason and beheaded. Rose leaned in closer and read the entry in Wikipedia: *Lady Jane Grey had an excellent humanist education and a reputation as one of the most learned young women of her day.*

"A lot of good that did her!" Rose muttered. *Doesn't exactly pay to be a humanist among savages,* she thought. She read on. The first victim of Queen Mary's burning was John Rogers, in February 1555. Rose knew that when she was last at Greenwich Palace, it had been July 6, 1553. The first burnings were then two years off. But time was never exactly synced up. Time behaved differently in that other world. When she returned to England, a year might have passed, or perhaps only a week. One never knew. She could pop up in Greenwich for Easter or perhaps Hampton Court for Christmas in an entirely different year—say, 1554, or, most dreadfully, 1555, when poor Mr. Rogers was burned at the stake. According to Wikipedia, by the end of that year, seventy-five more people had been burned. Maybe even her father or Franny! She had to get back. She just had to. If she could rescue Franny and her father, it would be worth everything. She'd sew that evil queen's clothes till . . . till . . . kingdom come, as her mom used to say. Her mother was fond of old-timey sayings—"anachronistic" ones. A word for next week's spelling review list.

She researched for a few more minutes and veered sharply off track from leprosy as she began making a list of Mary Tudor's likes, dislikes, and habits. She knew a lot that Wikipedia didn't know. Like that she went to chapel at least four times a day. That she liked her meat over-cooked and her eggs undercooked. Rose also knew with her twenty-first-century knowledge that undercooked eggs could cause salmonella, and salmonella caused diar-rhea. When Queen Mary was Princess Mary, she often was "indisposed," which was a polite way of saying diarrhea, or "runny bunnies," as her own mom used to call it when Rose got sick. So she made a long list of everything she knew about her "enemy," Mary, now queen of England. *I could be an FBI profiler*, she thought. But she didn't want to catch Mary. She just wanted to escape her. And the only way she could do that was to rescue her dad, and possibly Franny, and then never go back. As long as her father was in that century, she would not have a moment's peace.

The house had grown still. September had slipped out of the room. Probably back to her old haunts in the alley behind the house. September was basically a sixteenth-century cat. Social media and cat app games didn't interest this feline for long. Tomorrow was trash day. Might be good scavenging. Although fastidious like most cats, September could get into a good brawl over fish guts, and Rose sensed that the twenty-first century was a little too tidy for her. Fish guts, chicken hearts, and livers were ground up in garbage disposals and rarely flung into garbage cans. But the cat still prowled.

And so did Rose. She prowled downstairs, heading toward the greenhouse. There was a creak when she hit the second step. She hoped her gran hadn't heard it.

But she had. In her bed, Rose's gran's eyes opened. Rosalinda sighed, then murmured, "She's going again. Crossing over." She sighed a second time. "Godspeed," she whispered. It was not so dangerous when Rosalinda had time traveled, back in her day. Back when Mary's mother, Catherine of Aragon, was happy, happy as she had never been with Henry's brother, who then had conveniently died. After his brother died, Henry began his pursuit of Catherine immediately. Oh, young King Henry was in those days slender and jolly, full of wit and wonder. Ten times as handsome and lively as his brother. But then it all went sour. Poor

Catherine could not seem to bear a child, except for her withered daughter, Mary. Rosalinda had never encountered such an infant. The baby came out with a howl and a scowl on her face that she never relinquished. She was the grimmest baby Rosalinda had ever seen. Princess Mary seemed to have only two expressions—scowling and smirking. She couldn't help it, Rosalinda supposed. God knew they all tried to make her laugh. Impossible. And now Rosalinda's own granddaughter was going back.

Rosalinda was unsure, of course, whose reign Rose would wind up in. She never asked too many questions. She herself had served early in Henry VIII's reign. She sensed that her daughter, Rose's mother, had been there in the thick of the darkest days of Henry's marriage to his second wife, Anne Boleyn. And if things proceeded at that pace, perhaps Rose would skip a monarch and serve Elizabeth. Rosalinda knew, however, that Rose felt that her father was a man from that century. She most likely was right. But there was a certain unwritten understanding that neither Rose nor her gran would probe too deeply into each other's affairs in those old times. The times, after all, could not be changed. They were beyond their control. Rosalinda's job was in the present day, to raise her orphaned granddaughter to the best of her ability. And when she died . . . well, Rose would be left with plenty of money. But love? She had loved her as best she knew how. She would not make the same mistakes she had with Rose's mother, Rosemary, when she forbade her to return. A stupid thing on her part. To lose a living daughter through reckless stubbornness was ridiculous. That she would not do again. EVER!

Chapter 5

The
Virtual Rose

Once upon a time, *Rose thought as she stood in the greenhouse* and touched the hollow space between her collarbones where the locket had once hung, *there was a beautiful damask rose, cast in gold by my father, Nicholas Oliver.* She knew she was being rather dramatic, but damn that Princess Elizabeth, who had taken her locket. Taken it by her stupid Tudor right. *It's the Tudor Rose. Only a Tudor can wear it.* And with that Elizabeth had demanded it. Rose prayed that Princess Elizabeth would never find out that the rose pendant was not simply a pendant, but a locket. If she found the secret pin, it would open up. Inside were the two images, incomprehensible for the sixteenth century. She tried to imagine Princess Elizabeth looking at those photographs. The first one showed Rose and her mother at the beach, Rose in all her Disney gear and her mom in a swimsuit she used to call a mom-kini and the second showed Nicholas Oliver. He would be immediately recognizable to the princess.

Ever since the day Princess Elizabeth had taken the locket, Rose had missed the pleasant weight of it touching her collarbone. She missed it especially when she rode her pony, Ivy, at the Hunter Valley Riding Academy, where she took lessons. The thump of it as she cantered along was such a pleasing feeling. She of course worried constantly that Elizabeth would discover the pin and open the locket. How would Rose explain it? Although she had been just a child of five or six when the picture was taken, she was clearly recognizable. And what about her mom in her mom-kini? Had so much skin ever been exposed in the sixteenth century in a public place? And her dad, Nicholas, could also be in danger because of his appointment in the court. He'd be recognized and possibly condemned as a witch. Yes, they were still into that in England. Henry VIII's wife Anne Boleyn was said to be a witch, among other things, and then it was off with her head. Witches were gender free. Anyone could qualify.

A slant of moonlight fell through the cupola, casting the leaves of the vines in silver. A wind from nowhere stirred the dangling plants. She felt the moist, cool air of the greenhouse dissolve and a new odor take over. There was a sudden mustiness laced with camphor. Candlelit shadows danced on the wall. She was in the sewing rooms of Whitehall Place in London. There was no futon piled with ice skating costumes; instead she found twenty or more gowns suspended from a webbing of ropes. Gowns for the coronation that was to happen in a matter of weeks, on October 1, 1553. Rose had googled the date when she was in her home century. On that single day the queen would change her gown and robes half a dozen times. A gentleman who was opulently dressed walked through the forest of suspended gowns and robes toward her. His head tilted back as he poked at various garments. His name was Edward Waldegrave, the keeper of the wardrobe. A small man walked behind him. It was Simon Renard, the Spanish ambassador to the court.

"And Rose, you have sewn in the panel, yes?"

"I'm doing it now, sir." She looked down at the gaudy yard of white and gold tinsel. Had it not been faded with age, it would have looked exactly like the gown Elsa, the Snow Queen, in the *Disney on Ice* show wore. But this wasn't Disney, that was for sure. This wasn't an ice skating costume but a coronation one, and the queen wasn't Elsa but Mary Tudor.

Simon Renard came over to the table where Rose was sewing.

"Don't you feel that might . . . uh, spoil the lines of the dress?" Simon Renard asked.

"The queen insisted," said Waldegrave. "This was from her father, given to her on her first birthday."

Rose rolled her eyes. It was hard to imagine a father giving a one-year-old a more boring gift. *Oh whoopee, white satin with sparkles! Thanks, Daddy!*

"I feel it makes her look a bit old and maybe even flabby," Renard said.

Old, yes, thought Rose, *but not exactly flabby*. Mary was rather gaunt, but her skin hung loosely for one who was not quite forty. Dared she say anything?

"I . . . I tend to agree, Sir Renard."

"She wants it," Waldegrave said firmly. "She is our first queen in four hundred years, and what she wants, she gets!"

There had been queens before Mary, but technically Sir Edward was correct. Those queens only attained their position through marriage. But Mary was not married, not yet, though everyone was working on that as hard as they could. She was a queen in her own right. She was next in the line of succession after her brother died. At least twenty times a day people were reminded that this was truly the first queen in her own right. Mary herself wormed it into all her conversations. Her ladies-in-waiting commented on this fact constantly. Servants frequently mentioned it too. It was almost as if they expected a tip, a farthing or two, if they did it in earshot of the queen.

"Might it be ready for her when she comes for her fitting?" Waldegrave asked.

"Yes, sir, I'm just doing the final stitches now."

"Excellent, my girl. Excellent." Rose felt her shoulders slump. *Can you just shut up? I'm not your girl!* Which was worse, she wondered, Mr. Ross calling her "young lady" or Sir Waldegrave calling her "my girl"? She wasn't anyone's girl, except her dad's. Nicholas Oliver.

What was it with these guys—sixteenth century or twenty-first? *My girl . . . young lady.* However, there was zero chance she'd be pointing out Sir Waldegrave's patronizing tone.

Edward Waldegrave continued. "She shall be arriving momentarily in the blue velvet gown, over which she will try on the crimson robe of Parliament. That robe to the left." He pointed to a deep red cloak trimmed in ermine with tassels of gold silk. Rose vaguely recalled that she herself had been charged with sewing on the new tassels.

She began trying to calculate how long she had been gone from court. The last time she had seen the queen was in July. July 7, to be exact, the day after King Edward had died and Mary had made her swear loyalty. But time did funny things in this split world of Rose's. A month in sixteenth-century England might equal just five or ten minutes in her home century. The people of that old world never seemed to have missed her or registered her being gone. It was as if a ghost had served in her absence. Oftentimes when she came back, she had a kind of memory, almost like half-baked dreams. There was a familiarity with something she had been working on or doing while she had been away. Those feelings were seeping back into her now.

She recalled that relations between Mary and her half sister, Elizabeth, had begun to deteriorate. Mary had become suspicious that her sister was not attending Mass. Protestant services had been forbidden now. Ardent Catholics had condemned the Bible, as they felt many of the translations were anti-Catholic. It was rumored that Mary had sent out spies to report on any members of her court, from servants to ambassadors, who possessed or were suspected of reading the Bible. A confectioner in the kitchen responsible for all the sugar frosting on the cakes had been arrested for having been caught with a Bible. She also remembered that she had a new roommate, as her best friend Franny had gone back to Hatfield with Princess Elizabeth. She was now sharing a room with Sara, who had also been commandeered by the queen to serve in the wardrobe.

Then rapid footsteps could be heard approaching the sewing room. The door was flung open.

"Her Majesty the Queen is coming," a footman announced. Rose and three assistant seamstresses dismounted from their stools, came out from behind the sewing table, and fell to their knees. Sir Edward and the Spanish ambassador, because of their elevated positions in the court, were only required to bow deeply, then approach the queen and kiss her hand. Rose thanked her lucky stars that kissing that hand was not required. She just might bite it.

"Your Majesty, all is almost ready," Waldegrave said.

"Almost?"

"Rose Ashley, the head seamstress, is finishing the final stitches on the ivory gown to be worn for the banquet."

"Good," the queen said dryly. "You may rise." She directed the remark to Rose and the three young girls who were assisting her. Rose looked up and felt her blood congeal. There, hanging from Queen Mary's neck, was the gold locket. Her locket. The one Elizabeth had taken from her. The one made by her father. A feeling of nausea swept over her. This was worse, much worse than when Elizabeth had seized the locket. But how stupid of her not to realize that this would happen. Hadn't Franny told her, the first time Mary came to Hatfield, that she took things? Franny's words came back to her. *Elizabeth never wants any of her personal servants around when Mary is here. She even locks up all her jewelry.* Well, Queen Mary had already taken Rose herself. So why wouldn't she seize the jewelry as well? Her eyes fastened on the locket. But then she became aware that the queen's eyes were fastened on her.

"What are those things hanging from your ears—jewelry?"

OMG! My earbuds! How could she have forgotten to take them out?

"You know servants are not permitted to wear jewelry in my presence?"

She had to think fast. This was the first time ever that anything had really come with her when she had slipped from her home century to this one. She always arrived with none of her twenty-first-century clothing or "accessories"— barrettes or her iPhone, or sneakers. She was always period-perfect, dressed in her servant's uniform, the black kirtle with the fitted bodice and the ruff. Beneath the kirtle she wore her chemise, and on her head the French hood, which resembled something a nun might wear. Her hair had all been tucked beneath the hood. Not a hair must be show-ing—let alone earbuds! It was a mysterious change of cloth-ing. Rose never was aware of getting dressed, but she was always dressed appropriately.

"Answer me!" The queen's voice was pulled tight as a string. Her pale hazel eyes were cold and hard. The tip of her nose seemed to quiver, and it gave her entire face a feral look, like an animal tracking its prey.

"I am sorry, Your Majesty. These are certainly not jew-elry." She began pulling them from her ears. "They are merely drains, Your Majesty."

"Drains?"

"Yes, you see, Your Majesty, I am inclined toward ear infections . . . uh . . . my ears collect fluid . . . and . . ."

"Cider and garlic do not work?"

"Not very well." Rose was trying to imagine stuffing a garlic clove in her ear. "And of course it is very important that I be able to hear all of Sir Edward's instructions for the coronation gowns and robes. So I find if I wear these drains for a few hours a day, it does help."

The queen stuck out her hand. "I would like to examine them."

Oh Gawd! Rose thought. *What will she think? Wire wrapped in plastic. Plastic! It hasn't been invented yet.* But she rose up and handed the earbuds to the queen.

"What a curious material. What, pray tell, is it?"

"Actually . . ." Rose hesitated.

"Yes?"

"Um, actually, it's pickled pig gut that has been aged."

"Oh dear. . . . And you say it works?"

"Uh, for me it does."

"I would like to try them. My left ear has been troubling me."

"Well, of course you could, but I don't think it would be good." Didn't these people know anything about germs and contagious diseases (except for leprosy, of course)? They should. The sweating sickness had been so bad at one time that Franny's infant sister had died of it the summer before Rose had first tumbled through time.

"Why not?" the queen snapped.

"Germs?" Rose said weakly.

"Germs? What are germs?"

Rose clamped her eyes shut. How could she forget? In science class just last week, they had looked though their microscopes at some slides of bacteria. Ms. Lafferty had told them that Louis Pasteur only discovered the link between germs and diseases in the 1860s. "Before that people knew that disease could spread, but they didn't know the mechanism by which it spread." Ms. Lafferty said the word "germs" was relatively new.

"Germs are kind of like seeds. You wouldn't want seeds from my ears in your ears, now would you?"

The queen's sallow complexion turned absolutely gray. She opened and closed her mouth like a goldfish. No words came out. Then her eyes became mean little slits. "How dare you suggest such a thing!" And she thrust the earbuds back into Rose's hand.

Chapter 6

Stuck Up!

I*t was just as Queen Mary was handing back the earbuds that a* page arrived. Dropping to his knee, he announced in a trembling voice that seemed to crack every few words, "Your Majesty, the royal goldsmith has arrived to consider alterations to the crown required for your comfort."

The royal goldsmith! Dad! Here? She had only met her father twice and now he was here again.

"He awaits you in the privy chamber."

Privy chamber! Privy chamber! Where the heck is that? Whitehall was such a sprawling palace. She had to find out. Perhaps she could follow the queen and her retinue as they made their way to the privy chamber. It seemed terribly unfair that the queen could see her dad whenever she wanted but

Rose had to sneak around. Well, she would sneak if she had to!

Little did Rose imagine that her father was having precisely the same thought. *Why do I have to invent ruses to see my own daughter?* Nicholas Oliver did not know much about fatherhood, but this much he did know—it should not be dangerous for him to seek out his own daughter. His own flesh and blood. He had tried to get a message to Rose's friend Bettina of his impending arrival so she could alert Rose. But he was not sure it had gotten through. He waited impatiently in the privy chamber, where a few of the queen's ministers were also waiting for her to sign a stack of documents and proclamations.

Rose, meanwhile, had come up with a perfect excuse to get into the chamber at just the right time. The queen had been wearing the blue gown, which Rose had only that morning made adjustments on. The reason the queen had come into the sewing room in the first place was to make sure it all fitted just right. Distracted by the earbuds and the ivory panel discussion, that had been forgotten. Just after the queen left the sewing room, Rose had turned to Sara and gasped, "Good grief! I left those pins in the back ruching of the dress. Her Majesty might get stuck by them. Which way is the privy chamber?"

"Go out, turn left into the corridor that leads to the

portrait gallery, then take another left at the end and cross the courtyard. If you run you can catch up with them."

It was at least a quarter mile to the privy chamber. When she burst into the room, the half dozen or so people within looked up in astonishment at the flush-faced young girl. She immediately dropped to her knees.

"Forgive me, Your Majesty, but there are still pins in the dress. Pray don't sit down. Just turn around so I can get at the ruching." There was a slight titter as almost everyone present had an image of this stiff, cranky old queen having her bottom stuck full of pins. Nicholas Oliver indeed almost burst out laughing himself, for he was the only person in the chamber who realized this was a complete fabrication. *What a clever daughter I have!* he thought. He could not take his eyes off Rose as she dropped to her knees and began to scan the back of the dress, but not before giving her father a wink that seemed to say it all. They would meet afterward. She was hidden now by the voluminous skirts of the dress, and no one could see that she was simply pretending to remove pins and had had the forethought to wear her wrist pincushion and stick the phantom pins into it.

"There we go!" she said briskly, and popped up from her kneeling position.

"You got them all, I trust," the queen said grimly.

"Every last one, Your Majesty."

"You are dismissed, then."

Rose left, and as she was passing close to her father, she tripped—just a bit. Her father caught her elbow. *OMG,* she thought. *This is just like the lunchroom, except Marisol didn't pretend to trip. She really did. And it happened because someone stuck their foot out. And that someone had to be Tinker Bell!* She knew it. "By the horse guards. Blacksmith yard," she whispered as her father helped her stay on her feet.

A quarter of an hour later, she heard footsteps against the paving stones. She peeked out from around the corner, near the posts where the horses were tethered when the blacksmith shod them. No horse stood between the posts. The yard was completely empty, and the only sounds were the occasional neighs of the dozens of horses in the stables.

She held her breath. Her father was a tall man, and with the low angle of the late afternoon sun, his shadow stretched long across the paving stones of the blacksmith yard.

"Dad!" she called out softly. The advancing shadow stopped and she streaked across the yard, leaping over the shadow of his head and into his arms. The rough cloth of his jerkin rubbed her cheek and then there was the familiar scent of rosemary. He always wore a sprig of the herb in his waistcoat in honor of her mom, whose name was Rosemary.

"Oh, Dad!"

"Rosie! Rosie!"

"Dad, come back with me."

"But how can I?"

"I think I can figure it out somehow. I mean, I cross over. So you can too." They had had this conversation once before, but her father had hesitated. How could he fit in a century five hundred years from where he was? What would he do? Rose sensed those same thoughts racing through his head now. "Dad, you told me before that you would go with me to the end of time, to the end of space, and place. That you would cross oceans and borders—borders between centuries and between Kentucky and Indiana or Ohio or Michigan. Those were your exact words."

"I know, dear. I know that, and I meant it, but these are very dangerous times. You should not even be here. The worst is yet to come."

"I know that, Dad! I know better than you what is to come."

At that moment the blacksmith entered the yard, leading a large charger.

"Git yourselves out from the posts unless you want me to put a shoe on you," he shouted.

"We shouldn't be seen together," her father said quickly. "But darling girl, you need to go back. Soon. It's simply too dangerous."

There was no sense starting a scene with her dad here

in the blacksmith yard. Rose stepped back and thrust her hands into the deep pocket of her kirtle. She crossed her fingers. "If you say so, Dad."

"Really?" He looked at her closely. It was hard to guess what he was thinking. "You are no better a liar than your mum was." The trace of a smile crossed his face and the corners of his eyes began to crinkle up as if he were about to laugh. "Very clever of you, that ploy with the pins. Pins sticking into her butt!"

"Well." Rose shrugged. "She is rather stuck up."

"Is that a pun?" her father asked. She could tell he did not quite get it.

"I suppose," Rose replied. "You know, full of herself. Conceited. Stuck up."

"A very twenty-first-century pun, I imagine."

"Maybe not that new. I think the expression's been around for a while."

"As have I." Nicholas Oliver sighed.

"Dad! You don't look a day over forty-five. Honestly."

"That's five hundred and forty-five, in your time."

"No. Not a day. So will you come?" Rose asked.

"Will you go?" he replied.

"Outta the way now, you two. This is one skittish stallion."

They planned to meet again the next day if possible.

How would she ever sleep that night?! She was so excited. She simply had to persuade her father to cross back with her. She was sure her gran would love him. She and her gran together would figure out how to . . . to . . . to work him into their century. She was sure.

Chapter 7

Eternally Youthful

Sara and Rose shared a tiny bedroom stuck up beneath the eaves of York Place, in Whitehall Palace. York Place was the very heart of this sumptuous palace. It was to be the dream home of Henry VIII and Anne Boleyn, before he chopped her head off. Queen Mary delighted in ensconcing herself in its endless luxury. The shattered dream of the stepmother she could not stand. To Rose it seemed totally freaky. But that was Queen Mary—a total freak show if there ever was one. There was no end to her vindictiveness about Anne Boleyn.

"Isn't it all so exciting?" Sara said as she slipped into her nightgown and sleeping hood. She then leaned in toward the scrap of mirror they had hung over the washbasins.

"Look at us. Here we are, seamstresses to the queen, and now getting two washbasins and a mirror. We have status, Rose. Status!" Rose turned toward her so that both their faces were reflected. "Oh dear!" Sara gasped.

"What is it?"

"A wrinkle, I think."

"Ridiculous," Rose replied. "You're not old enough yet for wrinkles."

"What do you mean? I'm almost thirty."

"No, you aren't."

"I'm twenty-eight."

How could that be? Rose wondered. But it suddenly hit her—hit her like a ton of bricks. Sara *was* twenty-eight. When Rose had first arrived at Hatfield and they had both served Elizabeth, Sara was eighteen. The year was 1544, but now it was almost ten years later in Sara's time. It was 1553. She had to tread very carefully here. And just as she was thinking that, Sara said, "Look at you, Rose. You haven't changed a bit since you first came here. No wrinkles, just the occasional spot. I thought you would have outgrown those by now." She sighed. "You seem eternally youthful."

"Oh . . . er . . . I'm sure it will catch up with me when I'm least suspecting it." Rose forced a laugh.

"Well, we'd better get to sleep. We have the third banqueting gown to work on tomorrow." She gave another sigh. "She's such a joy to work for." She turned on her side.

"Who?"

"The queen, of course."

A joy to work for. She must be nuts!

"I do worry about her, though. Her health. So frail. And she's so thin."

"Do you think she has an eating disorder?"

"What? What are you talking about, Rose? I've never heard of such a thing—an eating disorder?"

"Never mind."

"Well, I just wonder if she's too frail to bear a child."

"I think she should bear a husband first," Rose said.

"Rose!" Sara sat straight up in bed. "That is a shocking thing to say. What are you talking about?"

"I mean, she needs to get married. Being a single parent and raising a child is no picnic." *I should know. That's why I'm here to see my father again now that my mom, the single parent, is dead.*

"Rose!" Sara giggled. "You have the oddest way of putting things. They are looking for a husband for her, Rose."

That was the understatement of the year! Rose thought. Talk about a manhunt. There'd never been one like this. It was the topic of conversation throughout the palace. There were all sorts of rumors as to who might be a contender for the hand of the queen of England. There was Charles V, the Holy Roman Emperor, then his cousin Felipe, prince of Spain, said to be rising in popularity in the court. And

Edward Courtenay, Earl of Devon—a real slimeball in Rose's mind, though she hadn't ever seen the others.

"All I'm saying is it's best to have a husband before having a child."

"What you are saying is scandalous, Rose. Of course she will have a husband, and they will live happily ever after and bear many children."

But, thought Rose, *the real question is not whether Queen Mary can bear children but whether a husband can bear Queen Mary.*

She soon heard the soft snores of Sara. She wished Franny were here. She wished her dad would come across with her! He was here in London, in Whitehall, and yet she had never felt so alone. Loneliness, she thought, was like an impenetrable stone wall that grew up around a person, cutting them off from everything. She suddenly realized that she'd seen or felt that loneliness in Marisol. She saw it in her large liquid brown eyes. Why did Marisol have walls up? And now she was sure that Jenny, aka Tinker Bell, had tripped her on purpose. Probably part of the initiation ritual into the twenty-first-century Mean Queens. Their special ops unit of wrath and destruction. You always had to prove yourself. They had done that with Sibby Huang when they put her up to sabotaging Joe's skates. But Sibby had thankfully realized how awful they were and how awful she had been. Now she wouldn't go near them.

There was so much Rose could never talk about with

Sara, but she could with Franny. What would Sara think if Rose had replied that of course she hadn't changed. *You see, Sara, I haven't really grown any older from when you last met me. Perhaps a few minutes at most.* But she couldn't say any of this.

But Franny knew all her secrets, because Franny too was a time traveler. She knew where Rose came from. She had tried to help Rose find her father in the first place. Franny would never betray her. Bettina, the dwarf, also knew who Rose's father was, but not that she was a traveler. Bettina was a good person. She had delivered *the* message to Rose, the one telling her to go to the garden at Hampton Court at midnight, to meet her father at the circle of the damask roses. It was the first time they had ever met. Bettina had also been stolen by Queen Mary from her sister, Elizabeth, for her own amusement. It was absolutely terrible in Rose's mind that dwarves were considered objects for amusement in the court.

Rose thought about the scene in the sewing room when the queen had entered. It had been such a shock to see the locket around her scrawny neck. The damask rose that was the thread that connected them all—her mother, her grandmother, and her father, who had made the locket. It was gold, an inanimate object, but it was more than that. In her mind the rose of the locket seemed to wilt as it hung around Queen Mary's neck. Rose's eyes opened wide in the darkness of the small room beneath the eaves. It was as if the brightness of a dawning revelation were flooding through her. Mary Tudor, queen of England, might wear that rose locket, but she would never own it. Just as Elizabeth had never owned it. She touched the hollow of her neck again where the locket had once rested. She felt herself dissolving into a dream—or was it perhaps just another reality?

Like ships passing in the night, Rose was slipping into her dream just as her grandmother was waking. Something had disturbed Rosalinda Ashley. And she did something that night that she had not done in a long time. She got herself out of bed without calling for Betty, her caretaker, in the next room. Then, bundling herself up in not one but three shawls, taking her cane, she made her way to the stair lift. At the bottom of the stairs was her walker. She had sensed that another damask rose was about to bloom. It must be moved to the sunroom. "Now!" she muttered. The damask roses began to bloom around Christmas. Rose had been in charge of moving them to the greenhouse. But Rose was asleep now. She didn't want to wake her . . . for, she thought suddenly, she might have gone "a-wander." That was what Rosalinda called it when she herself used to slip through time, back to that other century. Rosalinda did not pry into those activities of her granddaughter. That really wasn't her business anymore. What *was* her business was taking care of Rose as best she could at her advanced age. But nevertheless, she wanted to tend to this damask rose that was about to bloom. It was a special one. It was one that she had grafted in anticipation of the birth of Rose's mother. To think that her daughter, Rosemary, would now be almost forty-five years old, if she were alive. *Time flies*, she thought. *Or gets all tangled up.* When she'd heard that Rosemary had been killed and that her own granddaughter would be coming to live with her, she had grafted another rose for this new Rose. It seemed proper. The hopeful thing. She, of course, had never told Rose—not yet. The cuttings for grafting could often fail. She hoped this little graftling, as she called them, would make it. But she would not know for a while. Their first blooms did not come for two to three years. Rose would be fourteen or fifteen by then! Rosalinda wondered if she herself would be alive three years from now.

She heaved herself out of the stair lift and grasped the walker waiting for her at the bottom of the stairs. As she began to move slowly toward the greenhouse, the air stirred around her like a tropical breeze. She made her way toward the graftling. It was a lovely time to be in the greenhouse. She looked up through the room's glass ceiling. She saw Orion rising through the cupola overhead. The tip of Orion's sword hung almost directly above the new graftling for her granddaughter, Rose.

"Don't you dare snip it off, you star warrior, you!" She giggled to herself. The graftling didn't look like much right

Chapter 8

A Bitter Wind

"*Oh dear. I'm just one of those doddering old fools talking to* herself. Ready for the loony bin, I suppose."

They looked across the seedling table at each other.

"You're no fool, Gran."

"And I guess you're just back," Gran said casually, and began poking at the soil in the seedling cup.

So she knows where I've been, Rose thought. The key word was "back." One didn't get back from one's bedroom. One came back from five centuries ago. Rose tried to figure out what to say. Did one say, *Yeah, and jeez, is that Mary a witch! But I've made good progress on her coronation gown.* But instead, she looked at the spindly little seedling that her grandmother was poking with an old chopstick. The seedling was tied to another chopstick. She and Gran collected them, as they were perfect for staking young plants.

"What's that, Gran?"

"Oh, just an experiment in grafting."

"What's the plant?"

"Uh . . . a new kind of . . . er, rose."

"Will it make it?"

"One never knows, now do they? So fragile at this stage. But speaking of which, you came back in the nick of time."

Came back. Well, thought Rose, she wasn't denying that she'd been "a-wander."

"What am I in the nick of time for?"

"Might you take that other damask rose to the conservatory? I think it's ready to bloom. Put it in a dish at dawn, of course. That's when the greenhouse ones always open up."

Rose picked up the almost-ready-to-bloom rose and transported it to the conservatory, a round south-facing room with arched windows that the sun poured through. It was also where they ate breakfast and lunch.

"What time is it?" her gran asked when Rose returned.

She was about to say, *What time are you thinking of? Central standard time, twenty-first century, or Whitehall Palace time, sixteenth century?* She jammed her hand into her jeans pocket and found her iPhone and the earbuds.

"Nine thirty." She'd only been gone four minutes. She wondered again why the earbuds had traveled with her into the past and the iPhone hadn't. It was a mystery.

"Nine thirty. I'm rather hungry. Are you?"

"Well, yeah, maybe."

"Don't say 'yeah,' dear. It's so sloppy." Rosalinda was fierce about grammar, enunciation, and proper word usage. "Do you think Little China might still be open?"

"Maybe. I'll check their website." Ten seconds later she looked up. "Yep, still open. What do you want?"

"My usual."

"General Tso's chicken?" Rose asked, then added, "And I'll have my usual—fung yung three treasures with shrimp."

"Throw in some scallion pancakes, dear."

"There, I placed the order."

"Can you tell them not to ring the bell? They can do that thing, can't they? Textualize you when they are arriving?"

"Text me," Rose replied. Her gran winced a bit.

"Sounds like a naughty word somehow. But I don't want to disturb Betty. She would 'freak out,' as you say. Now there is a great word! Who would have ever thought of transforming 'freak' into a verb? Lovely idea."

While they waited for the food, they began two new trays of seedlings for a season Rose's grandmother called almost-but-not-quite-spring. These seeds in almost-spring would be moved into cold trays in early March, and by mid-April would be ready to plant outside. Rose had just completed her tray when she felt her phone vibrate.

"It's here!" she said. "I'll go get it."

The Little China delivery truck pulled up to the curb. Rose opened the door just a bit as a harsh cold wind was blowing. She felt sorry for the delivery boy who was making his way up the walk, hunched against the bitter wind, the hood of his sweatshirt pulled up. He wasn't even wearing a parka.

"Oh, thanks so much," Rose said, taking the order.

"*De nada*, I mean, nothing."

"Marisol!"

"Uh . . ." A flash of fear like a comet streaked through her dark eyes. Rose set down the order and yanked Marisol into the entry hall.

"You're just wearing a sweatshirt. You're freezing."

"It's all right. Don't worry."

"It's not all right."

"Listen, I gotta go. Driver will be mad."

"Well . . . you can't go out like that."

"I'll be fine."

"Just wait a second." Rose ran to the coat closet. The driver of the Little China truck was honking by the time she got back.

"Here, take this." She handed Marisol the new parka her grandmother had just bought for her.

"No, I can't take it."

"Why?" The driver was honking louder.

"I can't explain. It would be bad."

"Why?"

"People ask too many questions." Marisol now tore down the walk.

Rose stood with the door wide open. She was stupefied. Who asked too many questions? Was she mad at Rose for asking too many questions? Or someone else? She picked up the food and brought it into the greenhouse.

"Aah!" Rosalinda said. "I can smell the General Tso's from here. Yum!"

The warm air of the greenhouse assaulted Rose. She suddenly felt a crushing guilt. She set out the food on some of the empty seedling trays. The howl of the wind wrapped around the cupolas, where the vines were suspended and jeweled with flowers. This was an unreal world in here. Warm, fragrant, safe, and tucked away . . . away from what? When Marisol had stepped into the front hall, shivering and frightened, it was as if she had come from another world. Blown in like a fragile leaf from some distant land.

"You look worried, dear. Anything the matter?"

"No . . . I . . . uh, was just wondering about that cat that is sometimes around. She must be cold out there tonight. I think I'll check the alley. I left her a pan of milk earlier."

"Go along. But grab a coat. Check on her if it will settle you."

"Settle me?"

"You look quite unsettled, dear."

"I . . . I just worry about lonely creatures in the cold on a night like this."

Rose went out the back door of the greenhouse. She hadn't bothered with the coat. She stood there shivering, with tears running down her face. She clutched herself around the shoulders and walked over to the garbage cans where she had put the milk pan earlier. The milk was frozen solid. But she wasn't worried about September. September might only have three legs, but she was a survivor.

Rose wasn't so sure about Marisol.

Chapter 9

Born
to Bully

Rose was in the last part of her report for Ms. Lafferty's class. "The most famous of the nineteenth-century leper colonies was in Hawaii. But in the twentieth century, there was a well-known hospital in Carville, Louisiana, with a somewhat more enlightened view of the disease. It was found that leprosy, or Hansen's disease, as it is now called, is not inherited and is rarely, if ever, spread human to human. One would have to have prolonged contact with a human who has the disease. Even then it would not be spread by hugging or shaking hands or sitting next to someone on the bus. As a matter of fact, the prime suspect in the transmission of the disease is armadillos, as they can carry the bacteria linked to the disease. But there are no armadillos in Indiana. Thank you very much." Rose sat down next to Susan.

"Great report," Susan whispered.

"Have you seen Marisol this morning?" Rose whispered back.

"No, but it's just second period. She's often late."

"Now," Ms Lafferty said. "I believe it's Brianna's turn to give her report."

Brianna nodded and went to the front of the room. "Uh." Her eyes darted nervously around the room and then settled on Carrie. "We have heard from Myles on cerebral palsy that it is not an inherited disease but can be caused by birth trauma. And how Hansen's disease can be spread often from special bacteria in armadillos, and that these bacteria might have been around in other animals long ago. I am not sure what to call the condition that I have explored, but I am ready to discuss if it is congenital, genetic, or caused by some trauma at birth." Brianna took a deep breath and there was a long pause. Her eyes now settled on Lisa. Ms. Lafferty looked a bit nervous.

"And what might that . . . er . . . condition be, Brianna?" Ms. Lafferty asked.

"Evilness," Brianna said. "Is evilness a disease? Are we perhaps born to bully?" There was a gasp from the class, and Ms. Lafferty's jaw appeared to drop to the floor. "Is being mean genetic? Perhaps a brain defect?" There was not a sound in the room. Just a thick, dead silence. "In a study done recently at Indiana University in Bloomington, Indiana, it was found that the neural pathways in the frontal lobe of the brain had deteriorated significantly in patients who had become abusive. And in a study with rats it was discovered that neural connections could be repaired not through surgery but through training. Yes, rats can be retrained." She now turned her gaze on Carrie.

When Brianna finished her report, the class burst into applause—all except for Carrie and Lisa.

"Wow! How do you explain that?" Susan said as the period ended and they left the classroom. "Is she repenting for seven years of bullying? Actually I was in kindergarten and preschool with her. So more like nine years."

"Right? Lucky you!" Rose paused briefly. "But Susan, I've got something else to tell you."

"You look intense."

"Yeah, intense is the right word."

"Wanna go into the girls' bathroom?"

"No, that is a petri dish of gossip bacteria—talk about transmission!"

"Where should we go?"

"The cafeteria. It's empty now. First-period lunch isn't for another half hour."

They went into the lunchroom. There were some lunch ladies behind the counter getting ready and a man sweeping the floor.

"So what is it?"

"Still no sign of Marisol."

"She does miss a lot of school."

"Yeah, you would too."

"Rose, sometimes you can be so cryptic. What are you talking about?"

"I'm talking about last night when Gran and I got hungry. Gran loves Chinese food. So we ordered from Little China."

"Yeah, they're the best. So what?"

"Guess who delivered the food at almost ten thirty at night!"

"Who?"

"Marisol."

"She works?"

"Yeah, weird, right? Who at Lincoln Middle School actually works, and late at night? And you know what else?"

Susan, who was very pale, seemed to turn paler. Her eyes opened wide behind her round black-rimmed glasses. "What else?"

"She wasn't wearing a coat—just this beat-up sweatshirt."

Rose suddenly grabbed Susan's hand. "Susan, it was the

saddest thing. I offered to give her a coat and she refused. Absolutely refused. It was like she was scared to touch it. She said she couldn't take it."

"Why?"

"I'm not sure. She said she couldn't explain and that it would be bad." Rose paused as if remembering something. "Oh, and she said people asked too many questions. And I wasn't sure if she meant me or someone else."

"It's all so mysterious," Susan said. "Do you remember when she got here?"

"Not exactly. I think it was sometime between Halloween and Thanksgiving."

"What kind of parents let their kid run around delivering Chinese food late on a winter night without a coat?"

"Maybe she doesn't have any parents. I don't, after all."

"You have your grandmother and she lives in a nice house, a really nice house."

"She cares about me," Rose said softly. *But no one must care about Marisol.*

Rose remembered the crushing loneliness she had felt in the little room under the eaves in Whitehall Palace. How desperately she missed her father and Franny. How she felt so completely disconnected from anything she cared about, and in her isolation she felt no one cared for her. But of course she could not say any of this to Susan. Marisol wasn't a time traveler—of that she was sure. How many could there be in Indianapolis? But she felt Marisol had come from a place far away. And Rose was sure she had come alone.

There was a sudden crackle over the PA system.

"Students and teachers, the blizzard that was predicted is cranking up. White-out conditions are expected by midafternoon, so we are having an early release day." A huge cheer reverberated throughout the building. "Buses shall be arriving within fifteen minutes. Parents have been informed, as many as we could reach, and there have been radio announcements. If anyone has a problem going home early, please talk to Mr. Samm in the principal's office."

They loaded onto the buses. It was wild out there, with great sheets of snow whipping through the air. Trees were bent and fire hydrants were quickly disappearing under pointy snow hats. They reminded Rose of elves. The bus driver announced that they would be taking an alternate route, as certain streets were closed until the plows came through.

Rose was the last of her friends off the bus. Indeed, just her luck, as the only three others were the Mean Queens. Brianna was in exile, in a seat as far as possible from the sisters in crime. Carrie and Lisa were giving her the full treatment. Putting their heads together, whispering, and casting withering gazes at her. Rose ignored them all and stared out the window. The streets were virtually empty.

One or two cars and no one walking on the sidewalks buried in snow. She wasn't sure how far she was from her grandmother's house when she spotted a figure trudging through the snow. The figure's back was hunched, as if not only struggling against the wind but carrying a heavy burden.

Some instinct overtook Rose. She was absolutely certain this was Marisol.

"Stop!!!" she yelled out to the driver.

"What?" he called back, looking into his rearview mirror.

"I have to get off." Outside in front of a store was an automated snowman mannequin, waving at nonexistent passersby as music spilled out. "Have yourself a merry little . . ." *Oh, shut up*, thought Rose. "I have to get off," she yelled at the driver.

"But this isn't your stop—you're down on Forty-Sixth and Meridian. This is Fifty-Sixth and Illinois. I can't let you off here."

"Yes you can." Rose had stood up and was already heading toward the door.

"Young lady, sit down this minute." If one more man called her young lady, she'd bust him in the chops.

"You have to let me out! A friend of mine back there is in trouble. My uncle's office is near here. He's a doctor," she lied. "I have to get her. She might die. Freeze to death.

If you don't let me out, you're going to be blamed. Let me out now."

Suddenly the door on the bus opened. Rose was as stunned as the bus driver. Someone must have pulled the emergency handle. But she didn't wait a second. She leaped out. It was actually a spectacular leap into a drift of snow. She began running, as best she could, for the snow was thick. She breathed a sigh of relief when she heard the bus's exhaust as it pulled away.

She spotted the figure of Marisol half a block ahead. It was uphill, and beneath the snow it was slick. She fell twice, slipping backward each time. But so had Marisol. Rose called out, "Marisol. Stop. Wait up a second."

"Rosa, what are you doing here?"

"What are you?"

"Going to school. I'm afraid I'm really late."

"School's closed. They let us out early."

"You mean no one there?"

"Right. Snow day. Blizzard."

"Oh." Marisol looked slightly confused. "Uh, in Bolivia school never closes except for hurricanes." She immediately looked alarmed. "I mean . . . Oh please, Rose, just forget what I said." Her teeth were chattering. And that darned mechanical snowman was still blaring its soupy song.

"Marisol, how far have you walked?"

"Oh, just a little way." Her voice was weak and gasping.

"A little way?"

Marisol looked at her. Her eyes were not focusing right. Suddenly she slumped over.

"Marisol!" Rose cried out. The sound of her own voice was ragged. The dang snowman was now singing his anthem. Frosty the Guess What. This was a living nightmare. Rose looked around desperately for someone to help her. The song grew merrier and louder. *Go to hell, Frosty, and melt!*

"Marisol!" she cried hoarsely again.

Was she dead? Panic rose in her like a flood of torrential waters. What could she do? Calm down. *Calm down*, Rose told herself. She cupped her hands and began blowing her warm breath on Marisol's face. She took Marisol's mittenless hands and started blowing on them as well. "Marisol!" she cried. She knew suddenly what she had to do. Call Calvin. Calvin, her grandmother's driver. She took out her cell phone and dialed. *Please, Calvin, pick up. Please!* she prayed. There were so many things she could not control in her life. She could not stop her mother from dying in that car crash. She could not find her father. They were forever missing each other in that other century. She could not avoid serving that awful queen, Mary, who would eventually slaughter nearly three hundred innocent people! But she could stop Marisol from freezing to death. *Calvin, answer the phone!* Finally she heard his scratchy voice.

"Rose, what's up?"

"Calvin. Pick me up at the corner of Fifty-Sixth Street. It's an emergency."

"Which corner?"

Rose looked around. Her eyes nearly popped out of her head. "The corner of Little China, the restaurant."

"Okay, I'll be over as quick as I can."

"Quick! Calvin, quick." She looked down at Marisol's face. Her tawny skin had turned bright red. Was she still breathing? Rose wasn't sure.

She had to do something fast. She peeled off her parka and ripped off her stocking cap. She put the parka over Marisol's chest, then the hat on her head, and finally lay down on top of her. She had to keep her warm. The entire time, which seemed to take hours, she talked to Marisol.

Marisol, you cannot die . . . you can't. She took off her boots, then peeled off her own wooly socks and wrapped them around Marisol's neck.

Soon she heard the crunch of tires. A door slammed.

"Good gracious, Rose, what have we got here?"

"Marisol. Her name is Marisol."

Chapter 10

A Shadow World

"She's coming around." *Dr. Seeger bent over Marisol, who was* murmuring in Spanish. He gently flipped one of her eyes open and peered at it. "Pupils normal. She's almost finished the IV bag. Let's see if we can get a few more sips of hot tea down her. Betty, can you help her sit up a bit?"

Betty came over and lifted her. Dr. Seeger, Rosalinda's doctor and lifelong friend, was almost as old as Rosalinda and looked as if he could barely lift the teacup he was holding. Even when he was not bending over, he appeared bent. His cane was propped up in a corner of Rose's bedroom, where Marisol had been put in the other twin bed under an electric blanket.

Now Marisol's eyes opened wide.

"Marisol, it's me! Rose." Marisol gave a weak smile.

"*¡Bueno!* Marisol," Dr. Seeger said, and patted her hand gently. "*Hace mucho frío aquí.*" Marisol's eyes were suddenly wary. She turned her head away. "*No hay nada que temer. Cálmate, cálmate.*" He now turned to Rosalinda. "Would you and Rose and Betty give me a few minutes alone with Marisol?"

"I want to stay," Rose said fiercely.

"Of course, of course. She should have her friend here. But I shall be speaking in Spanish."

"Charlie, I never knew that you knew Spanish," Rosalinda said. "I'll leave you two to it now." With Betty by her side, she left the bedroom.

Rose didn't understand a word that was spoken. All she saw was that Marisol was beginning to cry. Several times she repeated the words *No puedo nada.* Finally, Dr. Seeger patted her head. Then he bent over and gave her a light kiss on the top of her head. "*Vaya con Dios,* Marisol."

"*Gracias,* Señor Doctor."

There was a knock on Rosalinda's bedroom door. Although Dr. Seeger's waiflike body could not weigh more than one hundred twenty pounds, he leaned heavily on his cane. He took a deep breath.

"Well?" Rosalinda asked. He took a moment to reply.

"Marisol is what I once was."

"What, Charlie?"

"Undocumented."

"Undocumented? What are you talking about?"

"What some people call an illegal alien."

"She's a child. She's a schoolmate of Rose's."

Rose's eyes were going back and forth between her grandmother and the old doctor.

"Yes, and I arrived here—let's see, when was it?—1948 from Argentina."

"I thought you were German, a German Jew."

"I was, but my parents fled Germany just before the war, when I was a baby. They went to South America. Then I came here—undocumented, an alien." He tossed a glance toward Rose. "I know you kids nowadays think all aliens come from Mars. Not me. Not Marisol."

"No, I don't. I know about aliens and illegal immigrants. So that's what Marisol is?"

"Yes, but it's much worse for her than it ever was for me. She's basically a slave in that restaurant Little China. She pays them rent for her bedroom, where she is packed in with nine or ten other women. They take it out of her minuscule salary. She has to pay off the coyote who got her across the US border with Mexico, after a long, long trip from Bolivia."

"Coyote!" Rose and her grandmother both exclaimed.

"That's what they call the smugglers who bring them across."

"How did she get to the border?" Rose asked.

"She mostly walked." He paused. "Or rode on train tops."

"What?" Rose gasped.

"She came here to search for her mother. Her mother had left some years before to make money. And she did. She sent it home, but then the money stopped coming. She's not sure where her mother is. She thought maybe Illinois or Indiana. In any case, if she doesn't pay off the smugglers, they will take reprisals on the family she left in Bolivia—an aunt, a grandmother, and a younger sister. It's an impossible situation."

"Nothing's impossible," Rosalinda said fiercely. "Can't we get her legal status somehow?" This was one of those rare moments when Rosalinda's mind seemed to crackle with alertness.

"It takes a long time. You have to understand that these immigrants live in a shadow world. They cannot really engage in much of anything, for if she's discovered they'll put her in detention."

"Detention? Like prison?"

"Not quite as bad, but she won't be able to go to school if she's in detention. They don't allow that. And if there is one thing this girl wants, it's to go to school."

"Oh dear . . . oh dear." Rosalinda shook her head. "Well, can't we just pay off the coyotes and get her papers, a passport, and a blue card?"

"Green card, Gran."

"Whatever. Can't we do something?" Rosalinda said.

"You're going to need a lawyer. Sam Gold is good on this immigrant stuff. He might be your man."

"Mr. Gold!" Rose said. "You mean Susan Gold's dad?"

"Yes, I believe his daughter's name is Susan."

When Rose got back to her bedroom, Marisol was sleeping peacefully. Rose looked down at her. She was very beautiful. Her brown hair spread across the pillow in lustrous rippling curls like breaking waves on a dark sea. She had come from so far. And yet when she got here, there was nothing except more trouble and coyote smugglers and slavery!

So, thought Rose, *Marisol is looking for her mother, and I am looking for my father.* At least Marisol's was in this century and this country. *Whereas mine . . .*

Chapter 11

Happy
Snow Day!

*I*t *was close to midnight now. Rose could hear Marisol's even* breathing. It was a comforting sound. Cook had made trays for them and Rose had brought the trays up. Shortly after eating, Marisol had grown sleepy. But before that all she seemed to want to talk about was school. Her favorite class was math. "No words, just numbers and shapes, like in geometry."

"Me too," said Rose. But there were so many other things that Rose wanted to ask her. How had she gotten here? Where did she think her mother might be . . . and the coyotes? But she dared not mention any of this. Rose couldn't sleep. And she couldn't scrub the memory of that horrible singing snowman from her brain. It was as if he were taunting her in some way—not like the Mean Queens, of course. Their bullying went far beyond taunting. She thought of Tinker Bell tripping Marisol and the time they stole the batteries frorm Myles's wheelchair. Their special ops mode, as Joe called it. Nobody could equal them. But how had that emergency door on the bus opened for her? If it hadn't, who knew what would have happened to Marisol. She recalled Gran mentioning that a few years ago a homeless man had been found frozen in Holliday Park, in the "Ruins." The Ruins were an area in the park that had fake Greek and Roman columns and statues. At least Rose thought they were fake. It was hard to imagine how a real Greek column got from Athens to Indianapolis. But then again, how had she gotten from Indianapolis to sixteenth-century England?

The wind that had scoured the city that day had died down. But the snow kept falling. There would be no school tomorrow, which was Friday. An email also came from Mr. Ross with the word list for next week.

Dear Language Arts Students,

I know you will all enjoy sleeping in tomorrow and probably going sledding at the nearest hill, but if you can spare a moment, you might take a look at the word list for next week. So here it is.

But of course, school lets out for Christmas break on Tuesday, and if this storm keeps up, there might not be school on Monday either. So Merry Christmas and Happy New Year to all. And now here is your word list! Have fun!

Obsolete

Alacrity

Esteem

Ecumenical

Presumptuous

Exasperation

Analogy

Fluorescent

Conundrum

Apartheid

Happy snow day.

Mr. Ross

She got up and went to the window. Although it was a moonless night, the carpet of thick snow provided a canvas for the most lively shadow dance. The shadows of trees cavorted around those of the greenhouse cupolas. She cast a glance at Marisol and then at the clock—one minute before midnight. *I'll only be gone a minute or two in regular time,* she thought. But of course it could be a month in that other century, where time slowed. She climbed out of bed and put on her fuzzy slippers and a thick robe. *I have to find my father. You understand, don't you, Marisol?*

The greenhouse was crowded with shadows, but there was one that was lost among the others. Lost or perhaps camouflaged. Rosalinda Ashley once again had gone downstairs quite on her own. She was in a far corner of the greenhouse where the moon flowers grew. There was only darkness, a thick, impervious darkness. While vines and seedlings tended to their business of growing and germinating under the coddling glow of grow lights, the moon flowers were left to wait for the brightness of the moon, which had slipped away for this night. There were no grow lights on, no false moon for the moon flowers, just darkness. And buried in that darkness, Rosalinda watched her granddaughter, bundled in her robe with a parka over it and a wool hat with earflaps. She came and stood by the graftling. Did she sense it had been created for her? Rose must know by now that the damask roses were special. That they were somehow the symbol for this peculiar family that could pass through these labyrinths of time. Rose of course was a beginner. It was somewhat easier to go to that distant century than to return to the present day. It took a bit of practice. It was more of a meditative experience. One had to train one's mind. It was actually an art. And one grew increasingly agile with experience. She called it Mastering the Art of the Rose.

Rosalinda watched her granddaughter staring down at the graftling of the rose and thought, *She's leaving me now.* A fragile light seemed to envelop Rose and then she merely dissolved like a dewdrop in the morning sun—except there was no dew and no sun. It was pitch black outside.

Rose was standing next to Sara in the choir loft of Westminster Abbey that looked down on the Sanctuary where almost every monarch since 1066 had been crowned. Never a female among them until now. *That sucks*, Rose thought. The procession had started from the Tower of London, where Mary had been for the past few weeks, preceding the coronation. Rose remembered thinking how it was not at all what she had anticipated. At least not the part that the queen's entourage was in. The worst part was that when the wind blew in a certain direction, it brought the foul smells of the river. They badly needed a sewage treatment plant. But that would have to wait a few hundred years or so.

"You have your needles and thread, do you?" snapped Jane Dormer, the closest confidante of the queen and highest ranking of her ladies-in-waiting. No detail escaped her. Rose was nearly out of breath, for she had arrived before the procession and run up all the stairs to the choir loft.

"Of course, milady." Sara curtsied.

If someone had asked Rose to describe her job on this day, October 1, 1553, she would have said she was a kind of EMT, except it wasn't broken bones that she and Sara were expected to mend, but clothing. If there was a tear, they were there to sew it. If a hem ripped, they had a special kind of glue made from horse hooves to glue it back, which worked surprisingly well. It wasn't Velcro but very effective nonetheless.

"Thank goodness the oil crisis has been resolved," Her Ladyship Jane Dormer said. She blew out her cheeks slightly in a gesture of relief. Jane Dormer allowed herself very few gestures or moments of self-expression. She was a handsome young woman, a good twelve or more years younger than her mistress, the queen. But she was a most somber person.

"Oil crisis?" Rose said softly. All she could think of was the Arctic National Wildlife Refuge and that pipeline thing. *Dang.*

"The oil crisis," Sara said as Jane Dormer scurried down the stairs.

"Oh that, yes, of course."

"How could you forget, Rose?"

Indeed, everything had been topsy-turvy a week before the coronation. There was even talk of postponing the event. Holy oils that had been consecrated by the previous kings' priests were used for coronations. But Mary was suspicious of the oil because those priests were Protestants and she was a Catholic. She couldn't bear the idea of having such unholy oils on her head. "Heretical oils," she called them. So they sent to a bishop in Brussels for some truly holy oil. Until it arrived, everyone was—well, as Rose's gran would say, everyone had their panties in a twist.

"She's coming. . . . She's coming!" Sara's voice boiled with excitement. Rose too was excited. First came the families of the ministers; next came Princess Elizabeth. "There she is," whispered Rose to Sara, and clutched her elbow.

"Oh, I hope the princess doesn't make trouble."

"Why ever would you say that, Sara?"

"You know how she is. There are rumors that she's been skipping Mass." *Who cares?* Rose wanted to say, but refrained. And Sara was right, the queen had spies who checked on these things. But if Elizabeth was here, that meant Franny might be here too. And more important than anything was the notion that her father might have come for this great event. After all, he was the court goldsmith, and there was talk that many of the ministers would most likely be presented with medals and decorations of honor.

Rose and Sara crowded close, toward the very end of the rail of the choir loft. The choir itself had first choice, and there were at least fifty in the choir. They watched as two men in the green and white colors of the Tudor Court now led Mary to each corner of the raised platform, so all could see her before she ascended the few steps to the coronation chair. There was a blast from the court trumpets.

Bishop Gardiner, now the lord chancellor of Mary's court, began to speak:

"Sirs, here present is Her Majesty, Queen Mary, rightful and undoubted inheritor by the laws of God and man to the Crown. . . ." He blabbed on a bit more while Rose scanned the audience below for any sign of her father. Princess Elizabeth looked slightly bored but had somehow fixed on her face a "smize," or a half smile that was totally insincere, where only part of one's face was involved—the eyes but never the mouth. There was Elizabeth, smizing away!

Bishop Gardiner was finishing his speech. "Queen Mary, will you serve at this time and give your wills and assent to the same consecration. . . ."

She nodded and Rose presumed she said yes. There were no mics, of course. But everybody in the audience said, "Yea, yea, yea! God save Queen Mary." This was when Rose crossed her fingers again. She saw the new queen move toward the altar and then lie facedown with her head on a velvet cushion.

"Jeez, what's Her Majesty doing now?" Rose whispered to Sara.

"The bishop will bless her now." The choir was singing a song in Latin. Rose didn't quite catch the lyrics. Of course, she didn't quite speak Latin. She wouldn't start Latin until ninth grade. Then Mary began moving to the side of the altar where her ladies-in-waiting stood.

"Change of robes. I guess it's all fine, or we would have been called down by now," Sara whispered. When Mary returned to the altar, the crimson velvet robe had been removed and she wore a kirtle of purple velvet. The service went on and on. She was kneeling, rising, lying facedown, then up again. A sort of coronation aerobics class. The bishop poured some oil on the queen's shoulders. Another costume change. Then she walked across the stage in her robes of state. And at this time she received her symbols of power: the sword, the scepter, and the orbs that looked like miniature globes on a cross. Basically in Rose's mind these ornaments all said one thing: Power with a capital P. It was then she caught sight of her father. He was there in the shadows. There was another blast of the trumpets as the bishop placed the crown on Mary's head, the imperial crown of the realm.

Rose craned to see her father. She didn't give twiddle sticks about this queen. But her father seemed to have dissolved deeper into the shadows.

"Where'd he go?" She turned around to Sara.

"Where'd who go?"

"That man—the goldsmith."

"How should I know? I was watching the queen. Weren't you?"

"Yeah, of course. But I just caught sight of him."

"Him? You mean Nicholas Oliver." Just hearing her father's name spoken aloud gave Rose a deep thrill.

"Yes—him. I . . . I was just wondering."

"Well, he was around, I think, because there were certain problems fitting the crown to a woman's head. I mean, this is the first queen in the history of England. You know they want it to fit comfortably and not squash her hair."

"Yes, yes, I suppose that makes sense."

Chapter 12

The Art of Smugness

But nothing made sense. Or perhaps the only thing that did make sense for Rose was to see her dad again. He was here someplace. She looked down from the choir loft. The ceremony was over. Mary had risen from the throne, and with the crimson mantle re-placed over her shoulders, she swept out of the Abbey, twirling the brightly polished diamond-studded scepter. The scepter now caught the random shafts of light that fell through the stained-glass windows. A light sword of sorts. But Queen Mary was no Jedi warrior. No way. She looked more like a baton twirler at some high school football game. Her face was almost joyful, but it was spoiled by a tincture of smugness. It was the facial equivalent of milk gone sour.

Now it was on to the banquet hall, where more than one thousand people were seated according to rank. Rose and Sara were not at a table at all, but once again tucked away in a backstage area separated by a screen, where the jesters and fools kept their costumes and props for the entertainment. The jesters and fools sat on stools while awaiting their turn to entertain.

Rose spied Jane the Bald. Her head was painted gold. She pranced over.

"Oh! Jane, your head!" Rose gasped.

"Yes, dearie, I'm an orb! Like the one Her Majesty carries, and over there is the scepter." She pointed to a man on stilts. The stilts and the man were also painted gold. "We do a little dance together when the merriment begins. Can't get too close to the torches, though. We'll burn up."

"Burn up?" Rose said with alarm.

"Yes, this gold paint can catch fire."

"They should have laws about that. Are there no safety laws?"

Both Jane and Sara turned toward her with looks of dismay. "What in the world are you talking about?" Sara asked.

"Uh . . . er . . . well, I just think that there should be laws protecting people from such dangers."

Jane sighed and raised her eyebrows high so that her golden orb of a head wrinkled. "There will be laws soon enough, and God forbid they are transgressed. The fires will come." A dread began to curdle deep within Rose's stomach. Jane quickly twirled about and then began a string of cartwheels, cackling away like a chicken gone berserk.

Sara gave a little huff of disapproval.

"What did she mean about laws? Are there new laws?"

"Oh, indeed. The unity laws, some call them." Sara nodded with grave authority.

"Unity with what?"

"Our reunion with the old religion, with the pope. Just one religion for all. High time, I say." She gave a haughty little sniff.

"But Edward was a Protestant."

"Well, no more of that," Sara said firmly.

"Were you a Protestant?"

"Yes, when the ruler was. But I don't believe you can have it both ways. We need to let the queen decide now. And she wants just one religion."

"Isn't there room for many? Why can't people decide for themselves?"

"Decide for themselves?" Sara's eyes opened wide. "Are you daft, Rose Ashley? Everything would be willy-nilly! So disorganized. You of all people should know. Supposing you make a single dress using several patterns, stitch it with twenty different kinds of thread? Make it of fifteen different colors? It would be motley—like Jake the juggler over there in fool's motley."

Motley was the many-colored costume that that some fools wore. Rose glanced at Jake, who was wearing stockings with a diamond design in four different colors, finished off with a tutu and jiggling bells attached here and there. And then, to top everything off, a pointy hat! But Rose did not get Sara's comparison of this costume to religion. Not a good *analogy*, Rose suddenly thought, as Mr. Ross's word list came to mind.

Interrupting her thoughts on motley, there was the sudden sound of horses' hooves against the stone floor of the great hall. Rose and Sara both got up to peek around the screen, as did other backstage people.

There was a man on horseback in bright armor, with a soft explosion of ostrich feathers on top of his helmet.

"It's Sir Edward Dymoke," Sara whispered.

"He's a big deal, I guess."

Sara looked at her, confounded. "Big deal?"

"Uh, just an expression."

"From where?"

"It means he's a very important person."

"Indeed!"

And at that moment Sir Edward Dymoke unfurled a scroll of paper and began to read. "'Whosoever shall dare to affirm that this Lady is not the rightful Queen of the Kingdom I will show him the contrary, or will do him to death.'"

Every pair of eyes in the room shifted from the queen to Princess Elizabeth. All eyes except for those of Mary. She tried to cast her eyes down modestly, but Rose saw the smile. Like two fat worms, her pale lips stretched. The tincture of smugness spread into a genuine smirk.

At the same moment Rose felt a little tug on her kirtle. She looked down just as Bettina the dwarf from Princess Elizabeth's retinue scampered off.

Then she felt something in her pocket. "What's that?" Sara asked.

"A note." Rose had to suppress the yelp of joy that nearly burst from her. She read it silently to herself. *The court goldsmith requests the first seamstress to make an adjustment in the imperial state crown. He shall be found in the metals shop.*

"What's it say?"

"Oh, it's about the imperial state crown. Uh . . . an inside headband is needed so she can wear it with ease on Wednesday for the opening of her first Parliament."

"Now? You have to do that now?" Sara asked

"I guess so . . ." Then Rose remembered something her mother always said. She replied to Sara, "Ours not to question why, ours but to do or die."

"Oh, now that's very clever. Where'd you learn that?"

"I'm . . . I'm not sure. Some poem. Or something."

Her mother would often say this, but Rose wasn't sure if it was a poem. Her mom had been an English literature major in college and was often quoting poems and Shake-speare as well. He, of course, hadn't been born yet.

Rose started to gather her sewing things together to leave.

"But Rose, what if there is a situation? What if those fastenings on her sleeves give way? What shall I do?" Sara asked in a pleading voice.

"Don't worry. I went over them this morning."

"But what if?"

"Oh, I don't know. Ask Her Ladyship Jane Dormer," Rose said.

She then turned to Jane the Bald. "Jane, I can't walk out there, not into the banqueting hall. I have to get to the goldsmith, to work on the imperial crown. He's in the metals shop in the Jewel Tower, other side of the courtyard. Everyone will see me."

"Not to worry. Everyone is supposed to see me. I'll be a distraction. Just cut across at those first pillars of the colon-nade. Once you're there, you can get out to the courtyard with no one seeing you. A fool can go anywhere. No ques-tions asked." She winked at Rose with her good eye. The other bulged slightly.

"Thank you, Jane, and don't get too close to any flam-ing torches."

"Let's hope not." But this was not a fool's voice. It was cold. Deadly cold, as if the blood in her veins had frozen to ice. She did not move for several seconds and her bulging eye, which usually was jittering about, froze as well. It was an awful moment.

"I'd best run along," Rose said.

"You'd best," Jane echoed, then sprang out from behind the screen and turned three quick cartwheels. Someone shouted out, "Show 'em your drawers, girl."

"I'll wear your trousers to my bed! And put my drawers on my head!" Jane yelled back.

People cheered wildly.

Rose scooted off and began streaking toward the shadowy gallery behind the columns that encircled the main dining area. She dodged between footmen bearing trays laden with roasted swans, their wings reattached, feathers and all! A culinary practice she found horrifying. There were long planks on which enormous roasted pigs were being carried with apples stuffed in their mouths and little roasted baby piglets surrounding them as if nursing! The whole banquet was a vegetarian's nightmare.

She turned the corner and was at least out of the way of the traffic from the kitchens when she spotted two shadows entwined behind a pillar. One shadow was speaking.

"Oh, I just want to kiss you, my darling. Kiss you and kiss you and don't make me cry, milady, don't make me lie, milady."

Rose slowed down. The man, whoever he was, almost

seemed to be singing. And the melody, the beat, and even the lyrics were awfully close to BWB, Boyz Will Be Boyz, and the adorable Yuu Park. Yuu's song began to stream through her own head. She might as well have had her earbuds in. . . . *"I just want to make out with you. I want to make time with you. I want to be true to you and only you. Don't make me cry, girl. I just want to sigh, girl. I don't want to lie."*

Park wouldn't be around for another four hundred fifty years or so. How had this happened? Then she heard a big sloppy smooch and the couple stepped away from the shadow cast by the column and stood in the light of a dim lantern.

Rose pressed herself up flat against the gallery wall. She could not believe what she had just seen. It was Edward Courtenay, the Earl of Devon, on the short list of potential husbands for Mary—well, kiss that goodbye, Rose thought. But almost as surprising was the object of the earl's affections—the recipient of the sloppy kisses was none other than Lady Margaret Carrington, otherwise known (at least to Rose) as Snail Head because of her hairdo in a style called coquillage, *coquille* being the French word for "snail." Rose thought it was the ugliest hairstyle she had ever seen, for Lady Margaret's bangs had been twisted into little snail shapes that marched across her forehead.

She had heard a rumor that Snail Head had left the service of Princess Elizabeth to be a lady-in-waiting for Mary, but what about all this smooching? Well, she couldn't stand here and wonder. She had to get to the metals shop in the Jewel Tower, where her father had said to meet her.

But now Snail Head and Edward Courtenay were lingering, and there seemed to be no way to get away from where Rose was standing.

Then she heard a peal of laughter and something tiny rolled out from the dining hall close to the pillars where Snail Head and Edward were embracing.

"Oh, forgive me," squealed Bettina.

"You . . . you loathsome dwarf." Snail Head spat out the words. She actually bent down, picked up Bettina, and began shaking her like a rag doll. Rose gasped as she watched this and then saw the shadow of Edward Courtenay quickly slide away—like a rat off a sinking ship.

"What did you see?!" Snail Head hissed like viper now.

"Nothing, milady . . . nothing at all . . ."

Rose was stuck to the stone floor. She could not move, but she realized she must. This was her chance. Bettina's eyes were looking wildly around as if searching for her. She had created this disruption at her own risk, to provide a cover for Rose.

Rose charged out from where she stood. She was now in the cool autumn air. No sooner had she crossed the courtyard than she felt herself being grabbed from behind.

"I saw nothing, my lord, er, earl . . ." Oh, it was so

confusing what one was supposed to call people with all these titles. "I saw nothing."

But when she turned around she saw it was not the Earl of Devon at all.

"Dad!"

Ominous
Signs

Chapter 13

A Proper Head for a Proper Crown

"*Oh, Dad!*" *Rose gasped.*

Nicholas Oliver's face broke into a smile. His eyes sparkled with tears. She buried her head against his chest. His ruff scraped her forehead. It all felt so wonderful, the scrape of that collar, just saying his name. His smell. He smelled good and fresh. Nobody smelled like this in this century. She bet her mom had told him about taking baths more than once a month and maybe even brought over some deodorant. But she'd take him any way he came—smelly or not.

"I thought I was to meet you in the Jewel Tower."

"No, my dear, just a ruse." He took a deep breath. "You

have to get out. It's just too dangerous. Things are going to turn very bad soon."

"Dad, first of all, I'm not going without you."

"Me? How would I live in that century?"

"You would. I'd help you." They were back to the same old argument.

"No, you must leave as soon as possible. This queen spells doom. She's not right in the head, Rose. She's going to start the new religious laws immediately. Much sooner than anyone anticipated. They have already begun rounding up people."

"Rounding up for what?"

"New laws will be passed in a matter of days, wiping out the Protestant church, the Church of England that was created by her father, King Henry the Eighth, and then protected by the laws of his son, King Edward the Sixth."

"Dad, this is so complicated. What does that really mean?"

"The queen forces you to go to Mass, does she not?"

"Yes, but you know I don't take it too seriously."

"She might test your faith in a way for which you are unprepared."

"A test?" She thought suddenly of the French test and math test that were scheduled for next week. She hadn't studied at all.

"Just don't get caught with a Bible."

"Yeah, I heard about that."

"Look, my dear child, you must trust me."

"I do trust you, Dad."

"Then you must leave."

"It's not as easy as you think."

"What do you mean? Your mother did it all the time. You know, when she felt she had to get back to you. I hardly knew she'd been gone, really. It was as if she had left a kind of shadow behind. Gradually I was able to perceive the difference between the shadow and her real presence. It was as if . . . I can't really explain, but her spirit lived within me. But then gradually it grew thinner and there was only the ache of missing her. Finally I realized she had gone . . . gone for good."

"I don't want to do that. I don't want to be gone from you for good. And I'm not sure how Mom did it when she went back to her home century. For me it's harder. I'm good at getting here. But going back . . . well, I haven't mastered that. It just happens when I least expect it."

She knew, or at least sensed, it had something to do with the damask rose. She thought of that graftling rose now that she had been standing in front of, bundled up in her parka and hat with earflaps, when she had crossed over this last time. Her grandmother had told her that grafting a rose was very difficult. They could not be expected to bloom sooner than two or three years, and often failed before that. When she had stood there gazing at it, she was trying to imagine the graftling's rootstock poking, squirming down into the soil. She had clamped her eyes shut. A sudden terror streaked though her now. She could imagine a tiny, infinitesimally small viper burrowing into the soil, its fangs lusting for those roots.

"What is it, Rose? Are you all right, child?"

"Of course, I'm fine."

"The color left your face. I thought you might faint."

"Never. I'm not the fainting type."

"Look, Rose, there is absolutely no telling what might happen. How soon the raids might start."

"Raids?"

"Yes, raids, as soon as the queen gets her Statutes of Repeal passed. The acts that will demolish all the religious legislation that her late brother, King Edward, put in place. Then the raids will commence and those still worshipping in the manner of the Protestants shall be rounded up. The first Parliament is four days from now. And that is when the old laws will be abolished and the new ones of this bitter queen put in place. Will you promise me you'll leave as soon as possible?"

"Yes, Dad." She was tempted to cross her fingers and lie outright. But she couldn't do that to her father. "But I told you it might not be possible. And one more thing."

"What's that?"

"If I go, if I figure out how to leave when I want to, I'm going to figure it out for you too, Dad. You have to promise me you'll come if I can get you across."

He took her face in his hands and cradled it. His eyes were the deepest, darkest blue she had ever seen. She felt as if she were looking into a night sky spangled with stars, the faraway stars that knew nothing of time or distance.

"All right, my dear. I promise."

"Now what about the crown?"

"Oh, that crown will never fit properly on her. There is not a crown in all of Christendom made for her. Perhaps we can look to the future for a proper head. Princess Elizabeth, if she survives *and* keeps her head."

By the time Rose returned to the banquet hall, the dancing was about to begin. The dancers were arranged in two rows facing each other. The queen and Princess Elizabeth were squarely opposite one another. And to Rose it looked more like a face-off than a dance. They were glaring at each other as the pipes struck up. It was a vigorous French dance, a galliard, that involved quite a bit of leaping on the men's part and some mild hopping and skipping for the ladies.

Rose and Sara peeked out from behind the screen at the lively dancers. Jane the Bald's head was bobbing between the two rows like an airborne golden bowling ball. Every once in a while she would emit a cock-a-doodle-doo and fling feathers into the air. Rose couldn't help but think that it didn't take much to entertain these people. But the dance looked fun.

"Don't you wish we could join in?" Sara said wistfully.

"Yes. Have to say I'm almost having a major FOMO moment."

"A what?" Sara said. Her face crinkled in utter confusion.

"Oh, just an expression."

"Expression from where?"

"Uh . . . West Ditch near Twickenham." This was the village Rose told people she had come from.

"What does it mean—FOMO?"

"Um . . . just what it sounds like. Fear of missing out."

"I love it!! It's sooo perfect. Yes! I feel completely FOMO."

"Me too, totally!"

"Totally!" Sara said gleefully. "You really do have a way with words, Rose. It must come from reading so much."

"Not the Bible!" Rose said impulsively.

"Of course not! I would never suspect you of reading the Bible, Rose. Not ever, especially since we are in service to the queen."

Now the music began to die down and the dancers returned to their seats while a half dozen dwarves ran out to the middle of the dance floor. They began their own version of the galliard that included somersaults and popping into the air, turning flips. The audience went wild.

"Oooooh! Aren't they cute? This is my favorite thing."

"Really?" Rose asked.

"Yes." Sara's brow furrowed. "You don't like them?"

"I like them, especially Bettina, but I don't like making fun of them."

"But they're having fun," Sara protested.

"Are you sure?" Rose said.

Just at that moment Her Ladyship Jane Dormer rushed up to them.

"Quick, Rose. This is an emergency. That vile Princess Elizabeth stepped on the queen's hem and ripped it. Her Majesty can't leave the banquet table."

"Then how am I supposed to fix it?"

"You need to crawl under the table with your sewing kit. Just where the Duke of Gloucester is sitting. He's been alerted and has moved his chair over a bit to make way for you."

"But the queen is at the far end of the table from here."

"All you do is dash out to this near end during the next performance by Jane the Bald and Jester Will Somers. All eyes will be on them. As you know, Will Somers is the only one who can make the queen laugh. I'll give you your cue as to when you need to dash out there." Jane Dormer stepped closer to Rose with a piercing gaze. "You understand?"

"Yes, ma'am."

"Excellent. Now stand by me and I'll give you the cue as I said."

The cue was a sharp poke in Rose's ribs. She dashed out from the screen and slid under the table. There were, of course, the Duke of Gloucester's bowed legs. She'd recognize then anywhere. A band around the bottom of the breeches that helped hold up his hose. It was as if she had entered a forest of legs. Not simply legs but the voluminous skirts of ball gowns as well. Some had billowing flounces. Others were elaborately swagged so that the silks and satins seemed to crest like breaking waves. The hems were elaborately embellished with ribbons, laces, and lavish embroidery in gold and silver thread.

Some people had slipped off their shoes and some were playing footsie with their neighbor. All of their feet stank. As Rose neared the end of the table where the queen sat, she noticed another familiar hem. That of Snail Head. Both her feet and those of the gentleman next to her were involved in an apparently lively conversation. *What a hussy!* Rose thought, coming up with an old word her mother had sometimes used. Darn, how she missed her mom. If only they could have all been standing there in the courtyard, as she and her dad had been just a quarter of an hour before. Why did people's lives have to slide by each other, just missing by a nanosecond? Why couldn't she have gone back with her mom into this century? Could they have all lived happily, if not ever after, then just for a while?

The tear in the hem was quite obvious. She could mend it easily without disturbing the queen. When she was about half finished, the queen slipped off her shoe. Rose could see through the queen's hosiery that she had corns on her toes. They looked a bit sore, and Her Royal Majesty's feet smelled like the rest under the table—a damp ripeness, slightly mildewed. *So gross*, Rose thought. Perfect environment for growing mushrooms. Myles, her school friend, had done a science fair experiment growing mushrooms and gotten second place. She missed home. She missed Myles, Susan, Joe, Kevin, all her best friends, and she missed Marisol!

So as she stitched, she began thinking about the greenhouse. The moist air, the cool shadows, where things stirred and began to grow in the night. Her thoughts reeled back to the little graftling in the greenhouse. She imagined those fragile roots nestling deep in the soil. And then the stench of feet began to dissolve and the forest of legs vanished. The clouds of billowing silks and satins, the boiling talk interrupted by shrieks of laughter at jesters' pranks, all of that melted away into a blessed silence.

She was back, back in the greenhouse. The only sound was the murmur of the humidifiers and the fans that dispersed the warm air from the space heaters. She tiptoed over to the graftling. It seemed to be all right. She looked at the clock. It was now two minutes after midnight. So she had only been gone three minutes tops. The graftling looked just the same. She crouched down so that her nose was almost touching the cup. She heard a sound from the entry hall. It was the purr of the stair lift. Had Gran come down? She never came down in the middle of the night—not alone. Wouldn't she have awakened Betty to help her? That was not like Gran.

She waited several minutes now. If it was Gran, which it must have been, she didn't want to meet her.

After ten minutes or so, Rose went back into her bedroom. She heard Marisol turn over in bed and then yawn.

"Rose?"

"Yes."

"Where you been?"

"Uh, just got up to go to the bathroom."

"Oh yeah. It's so nice having a bathroom all your own."

"You had to share one?" Rose asked.

"Sure . . . Rosa, I mean Rose," Marisol said sleepily, then added, "With about ten or fifteen people." She turned over again and was fast asleep.

Ten or fifteen people sharing a bathroom! Rose thought. She'd die!

Chapter 14

The Blessing
of a Blizzard

The ping of a text message coming in woke Rose. She saw that Marisol was sitting up in bed, actually doing homework! A math sheet.

"Was that your phone or mine?"

"Must be yours. I don't have a cell phone," Marisol said.

"Oh." She almost said sorry. But that would be patronizing! She reached for her phone. The text was from Susan. It was 9:45. Early for a no-school snow day. She read the message. A smiley face and a snowman popped up. Susan had an emoji addiction. *Hey, coming to your house with my dad. Your gran needs to talk to him.*

Really? Then it struck Rose. She knew exactly what this was about. Marisol! Hadn't Dr. Seeger told her grandmother to contact Sam Gold? *You go, Gran!* Rose thought. Should she tell Susan that Marisol was here? Better not. Nothing in writing. She turned to Marisol. "We'd better get up. Susan's coming over."

"Susan? Susan Gold?"

"Yep."

"She's nice. But what will she think when she sees me here?"

"Uh . . ." Rose shrugged. "She'll think I invited you to spend the night."

"Oh . . . she thinks I'm such a good friend that you would invite me for the whole night?"

"Yeah, why not?"

Marisol didn't answer. But Rose felt a twinge of sadness. Did Marisol believe no one would become her friend?

Twenty minutes later there was a knock on the bedroom door.

"Come in."

"Oh, hi, Marisol." *Just "oh, hi"?* Susan didn't look at all surprised. Her dad must have told her why he was coming. "Your grandmother says she'd like you both to come downstairs to the conservatory."

"Conservatory?" Marisol asked.

"Just a fancy name for where my grandmother eats breakfast," Rose explained.

The conservatory with its arching windows and troughs

of plants in full bloom was like walking into a garden in midsummer—except for the huge drifts of snow outside. There was a fountain at one end, with Pan blowing on his pipes, where water came out instead of music. The damask roses had completely unfurled and stood like elegant sentries, ushering in the morning light.

Her grandmother and Sam Gold sat at the table. There was a basket of freshly baked popovers, a bowl of fruit, and a platter of scrambled eggs. Marisol's eyes grew wide with wonder as she took it all in—the food, the blossoming flowers, the trickle of the fountain. Rose felt a wave of embarrassment rising within her. She and her grandmother had so much. How could she ever explain any of this to Marisol, who had so little, even though they both were motherless?

Rosalinda reached out and took Marisol's hand.

"My dear. There is much to discuss." Marisol had begun to tremble. A wild, feverish light glazed her eyes. Rose felt as if she might flee instantly.

"It's okay, Marisol." Sam Gold now leaned forward.

"No detention!" There was a ragged desperation in Marisol's voice.

"We want to help you. Your problems are solvable. You just need a little help. No detention. We'll make sure of that."

"How?" Marisol barked.

"Sit down, girls," Gran said.

Sam Gold now turned to Marisol. "Let me tell you some good news, Marisol."

"Good news?" A look of bewilderment crossed her face.

"Indeed. Little China was raided last night."

"Raid." Marisol gasped. "There was a raid?"

The word reverberated in Rose's head. Her father's voice urging her to leave. *Look, Rose, there is absolutely no telling what might happen. How soon the raids might start.*

"Yes, they were raided. Wasn't it lucky that you were here and not there?" Marisol turned her head toward Rose as if to give silent thanks.

"But the coyotes?" she asked. Rose and Susan winced.

"That is going to be settled very soon."

"How?" Marisol said.

"If you give us their names, it will be settled. I already have a list of suspected coyotes."

"How?" Marisol said again. There was a staunchness in her voice.

Sam Gold looked over at Rosalinda. Something unspoken transpired between them. Rosalinda nodded slightly.

"Rose's grandmother is in a position where she can satisfy your debt to these people." Marisol looked at Rosalinda in complete bewilderment.

"Why?"

"Many of us have been migrants at times in our lives. It

is not a crime," Rosalinda replied simply.

"I am not a crime," Marisol whispered to herself, as if this notion was strange and exotic.

"No," Rosalinda said firmly. "You are not a crime."

Sam Gold leaned in closer to Marisol. "You see, Rosalinda will not simply pay your debt, but she shall also become your sponsor."

"Sponsor! I have a sponsor!"

"Absolutely," Rosalinda said.

"And school?"

"You have the right to go to school as soon as I file sponsorship papers. The blizzard is a blessing, I think. Schools will be closed for at least two days and then Christmas vacation starts. That gives me time to get the papers in order and file for you. By the time school starts again, I think you'll have all you need."

Rose grasped Marisol's hand. "This is so great, Marisol!"

A fragile smile played across Marisol's face. She then turned to Rosalinda. "Very nice of you, very good of you, Mrs. Ashley."

"Oh, you can call me Rosalinda, child. If I'm your sponsor, you can't be calling me 'Mrs.'"

"Thank you," Marisol said softly, and looked down at the napkin in her lap.

There was the ping of a text coming in. Susan pulled her phone out of her pocket and looked at it.

"Oh, it's Joe; he and the guys are going sledding. We should go."

"Neat!" Rose said.

"Want to go sledding, Marisol?"

"I only have these clothes."

"Oh gracious!" Rosalinda exclaimed. "Rose, go get Calvin. We have to get this girl some warm clothes. He can drive you if the roads are open."

"The roads to the mall are always open. Are you kidding, with ten days until Christmas? I don't think they'd close," Susan said.

"That's set, then; you girls go shopping. I'll give you my credit card. Do I have to do something so Rose can use it?" Betty had just come into the conservatory.

"Gran, remember, you already arranged that. I have my own now."

"And I," Sam Gold said, "will treat for lunch. But no Little China." He laughed.

"Text Joe back, Susan. Tell him we'll be there by two for sledding."

"Do you need Calvin to drive you over for sledding?" Rosalinda asked.

"No. We can walk there in the snow from here." She turned to Marisol. "We'll get you snow pants, boots, and a parka. And a few other things too . . . is that okay, Gran?"

"Of course—the child isn't going to sled every day from

now until the snow melts. Get her everything she needs—pajamas, underwear . . ." Rosalinda paused. "Cute outfits," she said with a twinkle in her eye.

"Oh, Gran, you really are the best." Rose popped up and gave her grandmother a big hug and a kiss. Rosalinda beamed.

"Is it hard?" Marisol said as they trudged to the top of Tenny's Hill at Marian Park, dragging the sleds they'd bought at the mall.

"Oh no, not at all," Susan said. "Look, there goes Myles."

"In his wheelchair?" Marisol said.

"No, Kevin and Anand help him out of the wheelchair onto that saucer, and he just slides on down in it."

"Hi, Myles!" Rose yelled, and waved to him as the saucer spun in slow circles down the hill.

"Hi!" Joe limped up.

"You got a snow-proof cast, I see," said Rose.

"I think they all are these days. But I can sled," Joe replied.

"Too bad you can't skate yet. Look, they cleared the ice on the lake for skating," Rose said.

"Let's get started," Susan said, then flopped herself down on a sled and took off.

"So fast!" Marisol said. "I don't know, Rose."

"Oh, it's fun. You want to go with me the first time?"

"How do you do that?"

"I'll just get on the bottom and you can be on top of me. I'll steer. Not much to run into, though."

Just as they were arranging themselves on the sled, Carrie and Lisa and Jenny, the sixth grader, came up.

"Well, look who's here!" Carrie drawled.

"Who?" snapped Rose. Jenny's hair was pink, just like Lisa's.

"Our leetel *amigo*." She began speaking in an exaggerated Spanish accent. "Where you been, Marisol?"

"None of your business, Carrie. Don't pay any attention to them, Marisol," Rose muttered, and shoved off.

She heard Marisol give a squeal as the sled sailed down and felt her grip her shoulders tight. The cold bit their faces but Marisol was laughing all the way.

"So fast!" Marisol gasped as they slowed to a stop. "I can do it by myself. I think." She walked to the top pulling the sled, and saw Myles.

"Hi, Myles!" Marisol said. "Did you see us?"

"Sure did." Anand and Kevin were pulling him on his saucer up to the top of the hill.

Carrie's words rang in her ears. She had to admit what Carrie said rattled her. She hoped that Sam Gold could get those papers going and Gran could become Marisol's sponsor soon. She was relieved not to see them when she was back at the top of the hill.

Susan came up to them. "How'd you like it, Marisol?"

"I loved it. No snow in Bolivia." She went over and took the third sled they had brought, flopped onto it, and started down the hill like a pro. Susan started to go toward her sled.

"Wait a minute, Susan," Rose called out.

"You look worried. Something wrong?" Susan said.

"Not sure. It's just Carrie and Lisa and Jenny."

"Oh yeah, Jenny seems to have replaced Brianna. So what?"

"They came up and . . ." Rose repeated Carrie's teasing remark.

"She said that?"

"Yep, and it worries me."

"Oh, I wouldn't worry. They just need a new target now that they got in trouble with Joe's skating accident."

"But that's just the problem. Don't you see? Marisol can't afford to be their target. She's . . . she's really vulnerable."

"Yeah, but you know my dad's working on it."

"How fast do you think he can get those papers and get Gran to be her sponsor?"

"I don't think it should take that long."

"I hope not," Rose said.

"Look, here comes Marisol up the hill. For someone who had hypothermia yesterday, she sure is making a fast recovery. She's tough."

"Yeah," Rose said, thinking of what Dr. Seeger had said about Marisol walking or riding on train tops all the way here. *Yeah, she's tough, all right.*

The shadows grew longer. Down by the lake some families had built a fire in the firepit. Rose, Marisol, and Susan dragged their sleds toward it. A man was poking the logs a bit and looked up as the girls approached. It was their homeroom teacher, Mr. Ross. "Oh, I see you're all here studying the word list for the test! Want some hot chocolate?"

"Sure," Susan said. "Uh . . . with *alacrity*, Mr. Ross."

"Oh my goodness, extra points for that!" He laughed. They sat on stumps with perhaps a dozen other people, sipping the hot chocolate from paper cups.

"Look at that!" One mother with a young child on her lap pointed toward the lake. Someone was skating across in long sweeping backward strides. The skater lifted her back foot from the ice; then, springing from her forward leg, she shot straight up into the air and landed as softly as a downy feather. Her own shadow stretched out across the lake. Quiet fell on the circle of people warming themselves by the fire as they watched, mesmerized by the skater. She was like a liquid diamond cutting figures in the ice.

"It's Brianna." Joe sighed. "She's such a beautiful skater."

"With a twisted heart," Susan said grimly. For it was Brianna who had been behind the sabotage of Joe's skates, causing him to fall and break his ankle so he couldn't skate in the Snow Show. Of course, Brianna herself had been banned from the Indianapolis Skating Club.

"She has no place else to skate, I guess," Joe said. His voice had a slight tinge of sadness.

"She got what she deserved," Rose said.

Brianna skated on and on, not seeming to be aware in the least of the people who were watching her. She appeared to be wrapped in a hidden music that only she could hear, in a magical dream of frost and late-afternoon shadows.

Chapter 15

The Longest
Night

There were many more days of sledding and going to movies. She and Marisol had gone and picked up a Christmas tree with Calvin. He set it up in the library and together they decorated it. Her grandmother watched them while sipping a glass of sherry—just one glass on these cold winter nights. She called it her winter constitutional. She seemed somewhat more distracted than usual and she began humming a song.

"Lovely song, Mrs. Ashley—I mean Rosalinda," Marisol said as she hung up a glittering silver ball. "What's it called?"

"'Greensleeves.' Very old song. Oh, you should have heard him sing it."

"Him?" Rose asked.

"Henry, to Anne Bo . . ." Rose flashed her grandmother a terrified look. She sensed in an instant what she had been about to say. Henry VIII to Anne Boleyn. Somehow she knew that he was the composer of this song. Perhaps Princess Elizabeth had mentioned it. Her grandmother had spoken only once of the times she had "gone a-wander." That was several weeks before Christmas, when Rosalinda had been in the hospital. She had confessed that Rose, like herself, had the gene. *You see, you got the gene. . . . Richmond was my first visit. Hung about there for quite a while.*

My mom had the gene too, I think, Rose had replied.

Yes, she did. It's why she and I had a falling out. I tried to stop her from going back. All I could imagine for her was heartbreak. It was a mistake. And so her grandmother vowed never to stop Rose from going back. *Rose,* she had said, *I shall love you through all time. . . . Through every century imaginable.*

But as Christmas approached, Rose felt an increasing tug on her heart. Her father. As much as she had come to love her gran, wouldn't it be wonderful to celebrate Christmas with her father, and to see Franny again? She had grown quite close to Marisol, but there were so many things she could not share with her, and she sensed that Marisol felt the same. But the one thing they had in common was that they both desperately missed a parent. There were times in the night when Marisol called out for her mother, restless in her sleep.

Rose became obsessed with the idea of celebrating

Christmas with her dad and possibly Franny, and on this particular night, sleep seemed impossible. She began to wonder if one of her trips back might ever be at Christmastime. When she slipped through time, there was never predicting the date she would arrive on. Not the day, nor the month, nor the year in that distant century. She tried to keep track of these two time zones as she slid between them. She even kept a diary. The first date that Rose had ever visited that century had been September 10 in her own century. She had fallen through that crack in time when she was in the greenhouse, high up in one of the cupolas checking on some jasmine. When she had arrived, in the year 1544, she found herself at Hatfield. It was midsummer. Not September at all. Possibly July, and the day was hot.

There were leaps in years as well. One year it might be 1544, and then inexplicably she would return three years later, as she did at the time of King Henry VIII's death in January 1547. Her method of keeping track of time was to cross out the actual twenty-first-century date in her own diary and write in the sixteenth-century date above it. She had done just that around Thanksgiving, near the time that Joe had broken his ankle. The date was crossed out and above it she'd written February 10, 1547.

She reread what she had written. *Holy smokes do they have weird funeral practices here. First of all, King Henry died almost two weeks ago and it's taken them that long to bury him—in parts, I might add. Yeah, creepy! His body was buried in Westminster, his heart and "entrails" in Windsor Palace. I'm not the only one who finds this creepy. Princess Elizabeth really freaked. She told her tutor and the chief steward of her household no way, Jose, though she didn't quite use those words.*

But I have to say the mourning clothes are totally cool. As soon as I got back, I made some sketches of some of the best outfits. My favorites were the cone sleeves that a lot of the women wore. The Duchess of Somerset was the classiest at the funeral. Too bad I didn't have my iPhone, but here's a picture of her I found on Wikipedia. I'm going to post these on my blog, and some other pictures I found on Wikipedia too.

Rose tiptoed to her laptop and clicked on her blog, *Threads*, and looked up her posts on mourning clothes.

A passing interest of mine is sixteenth-century mourning clothes. Take a look at those sleeves and the big fat pearls that the Duchess of Somerset is wearing. Pearls were very in back then. A symbol of chastity. Ha! There were rumors about the Duchess of Somerset. Let's just say she got around.

And on Pinterest I found some more pictures of mourning clothes. Here are my two favorites. The first dress shows the cone sleeve, lined in gold cloth. I'm crazy about cone sleeves. The second is very Batwoman. I love it! Very fashion forward for the age.

Clothes to Die For

Rose crawled back into bed. It was almost midnight. In another minute it would be December 21, and the shortest day and the longest night of the year would begin. The winter solstice. The North Pole would tilt toward the sun and a new cycle of light would commence. She looked at the window. This was the first night it hadn't snowed heavily since the blizzard. It was a crystalline winter night. The moon was no more than an eyelash. The utter blackness of the sky had become like a Christmas tree for the ornaments of the constellations. It reminded her of the night that she had stood in the courtyard of Westminster Palace and her father had cradled her face in his hands so gently. She knew that she had to go back. Christmas or not. It was as if she herself were being tilted toward a night that only existed almost five centuries ago.

At 12:01 on this longest night she once again put on her robe and fuzzy slippers and tiptoed down to the greenhouse. She stood in front of the graftling and studied it. She tried again to imagine its roots. She tried to imagine its life three years from now when its first buds might open up and the petals unfurl—unfurl perhaps in the distant dawn of midsummer's longest day, a day that would spill with light.

Chapter 16

They Burn Witches Here, Don't They?

"*They say she has accepted him.*"

"He's at least ten years younger!"

OMG, Rose thought. *All this again!* That's all anyone talked about—when the queen would decide on the proper husband. That, and would Queen Mary put her half sister, Princess Elizabeth, in the Tower of London. The religious laws were becoming stricter and stricter. Rose was walking through the presence rooms of Beaulieu Palace. The presence chamber was where the ladies-in-waiting of the queen sat, just outside the most private chamber of the queen. She was not sure why she had been called. This palace, Beaulieu, was one of the queen's favorites. She had reclaimed it on the death of her hated stepmother, Anne Boleyn. In her spiteful way, Mary seemed to enjoy occupying it more than ever now that she was queen. She loved inviting Princess Elizabeth, daughter of the beheaded Anne Boleyn, to visit. "Inviting" was hardly the word. It was more like a command performance. There was no choice.

Rose entered the queen's private chamber. It was an odd scene. Simon Renard, the Spanish ambassador, was standing by a large portrait of a very handsome man. Three members of the queen's Privy Council stood by looking anxious. Queen Mary stood in front of the portrait, trembling, with her hand pressed to her chest. "Is it a true likeness?"

"As true as you'll ever see, Your Majesty. It is by Titian, the Venetian painter," Simon Renard replied.

At that moment Edward Waldegrave entered the room. "I've brought the swatches, Your Majesty."

"Can you have the gown completed by his visit?" All eyes turned toward Rose.

"And when, might I ask, is the visit?" asked Rose.

"Three weeks," Ambassador Renard replied. "That is, if the weather permits and the Bay of Biscay is calm."

Rose could feel Waldegrave's eyes boring into her. She of course had no choice. It could be nuclear war—of course, it couldn't really, as that would not be a possibility for several centuries—but nukes or not, the dress had to be finished. Rose nodded and softly said, "Of course, the dress shall be done."

※

The dress was almost finished and the Bay of Biscay was calm, but the queen had fallen ill. Rose of course was not informed until the last minute. No one was, except for the most intimate members of the court. Rose was just coming through the presence room with the gown, a sumptuous russet color called gingerline, trimmed in ermine at the queen's request. Rose had mildly objected to the ermine, fashion-wise—completely wrong move! But what could she do? The queen's fashion instincts were beyond bad, actually atrocious. There were more than five pounds of pearls encrusting the sleeves. Princess Elizabeth would never veer down this path of gaudy opulence. In comparison the princess dressed like a nun. She was of what Rose's mom would have called the "less is more" school of fashion. Whereas Queen Mary was of the "more is more" school.

She had taken barely three steps into the presence room when she noticed a thick pall in the air. Snail Head slid her eyes toward Rose and muttered something.

"No! She wants to see it." Lady Susanna now got up from the chair she was sitting in next to Snail Head. Her embroidery hoop was still in her hand. Susanna Clarencieux was the queen's favorite gentlewoman.

"Her Royal Majesty has fallen quite ill. The physicians are with her now. The visit of Prince Felipe has been postponed. But it is felt that showing Her Majesty the dress might lift her spirits and hasten her recovery."

It was a strange sight that greeted Rose as she entered the bedchamber. There were several people in the room. Some she recognized, others she didn't. There of course was Ambassador Renard. The lord chancellor was pacing up and down the royal bedchamber. The portrait of handsome Prince Felipe was propped a few feet from the bed. And Jane the Bald was performing what were called "gentle antics" for the sick queen's amusement, perching herself in odd places and making an assortment of bird sounds, then performing a cartwheel or two. This seemed odd to Rose, but she supposed that since there was no television, a fool like Jane the Bald was as good as any entertainment. She could recite a nonsense poem, turn a cartwheel, and imitate all sorts of animals. One of the most frequent commands that could be heard coming from Queen Mary was "Send for the fool! I need to laugh." And Jane the Bald would almost instantly materialize.

Most surprising to Rose was to see Edward Courtenay standing beside the portrait, handsomely dressed as if not for the sick room but for a grand occasion. He was almost posing. Was he actually trying to court the queen in some way? Hadn't it been decided that Prince Felipe of Spain was to be the husband Mary had selected to share her throne? *Hey, you lost*, Rose thought. *Go back to Snail Head.* The lord chancellor flashed Courtenay a sharp look.

Two men whom Rose did not recognize hovered over the bed. Then one with his back turned suddenly called out, "Basin!"

Jane Dormer rushed forward with a metal basin, her own maid, Daisy, beside her. When Daisy passed by Rose, Jane Dormer hissed, "For God's sake, step back, child." Rose looked at the basin in horror. There was at least a cup of blood sloshing about in the bottom.

"What in the world," Rose whispered to herself.

"Don't look." It was Jane the Bald, who was now beside her and grasped Rose's elbow as if to steady her.

"What is this?"

"Never seen anyone bled before?"

"Uh, not on purpose."

"Bloodletting is a treatment. Does wonders for the humors."

"There is absolutely nothing funny about this!" Rose said, her eyes wide with horror.

"The humors, my dear. It keeps them in balance." Rose blinked and shook her head in dismay. "Really, child, where are you from that you've never seen bloodletting?"

"Never seen it."

"It can cure everything, from spots on your face to pneumonia to gout and dropsy."

"Dropsy?"

"Swelling. Look at her hands—not the arm with the

vein where they are drawing the blood. The other one."
Jane suddenly stiffened as her eyes fell on Edward Courtenay. Then she gave a muffled little chirp. "Time for a somersault, I believe." She squatted on the floor, and Rose heard the thump of a somersault follow.

What is he doing? Rose wondered. Edward Courtenay had now picked up the hand of the queen and was stroking it. She was about to ask Jane what it meant. But in a split second Jane had seemed to somersault away into thin air. Rose couldn't imagine where she had gone so quickly.

Edward Courtenay was now leaning close to the queen's ear, whispering. She looked dreadful, but a fragile smile seemed to struggle from the corners of her pale lips. Even sick and with this smile creeping across her face, Mary Tudor looked mean in Rose's eyes. A nasty piece of work, as her grandmother Rosalinda might say. The lord chancellor was having none of it.

"Your Majesty, Rose Ashley the seamstress is here with your meeting dress," the lord chancellor said.

A sour look crossed Edward Courtenay's face as his mother, Lady Gertrude, let her eyes shoot daggers at the lord chancellor. Rose was suddenly paralyzed, caught in a crossfire of court politics and dazzling ambitions. It was dangerous. She started to take a step forward, then felt a heavy hand on her shoulder.

It was Lady Gertrude. "I think that would be

overstimulating, my dear. Much too exciting to see your meeting dress, let alone the wedding dress."

The lord chancellor came up and whisked the dress from Rose's arms. "I'll take that," he said firmly. Lady Gertrude turned a liverish color. Rose backed away.

"Basin!" a doctor called out.

Another basin was brought forth, and another cup of blood collected.

So much for dying in peace, Rose thought as she retreated from the royal bedchamber.

"Pssst." The sound was like a dart whistling out from the shadows. She had just left the presence room and turned into a corridor. "Pssst!" The sound lanced the shadows as Rose spied a tuft of dyed pigeon feathers.

"Jane!"

"Surprise!"

"Yes, how did you manage to get out of the sick room with no one spotting you? One minute you were there, the next gone."

"Gone? Not exactly." Her painted-on eyebrows shot up to that hairless expanse of her skull. She had painted a moon on one of her cheeks and a radiant sun on the other. "I didn't get out. I got under."

"Under? What are you talking about?"

"I somersaulted under the bed just while that TOD was

whispering into the queen's ear."

"TOD? What is that?"

"Turd of a dog." Rose was hardly surprised by this talk. The court loved bathroom humor. They might be masters of the sixteenth-century world in the greatest of kingdoms, but there was more fart and poop talk than in a second-grade classroom.

"Well, what was he saying? Still courting her, I suppose, despite Prince Felipe."

"Yes, courting in a manner of speaking."

"And just what do you mean by that, Jane?"

"I mean it was not exactly sweet nothings he was whispering in her ear." Her face grew rigid; the jittering eye stilled for several seconds.

"What was it?"

"In a word?" She hiked one eyebrow up, and her bulging eye flitted about as if tracking a gnat. Rose nodded. She felt a dread begin to creep through her.

"Murder," Jane said softly. "It takes a fool to know a mad queen."

"I don't understand."

Jane's face softened. She took Rose's hand.

"Listen carefully, dear child. I know not from whence you come." Rose started. "Calm down. You need not tell me anything, but I sense it is from afar."

"But this is murder he was speaking of, you say?"

"Soon." Her nose twitched. "I can smell the coals now."

"Fires burning?" Rose asked.

Jane nodded solemnly. "Mark my words, soon it will begin."

"But Edward Courtenay—how does he fit into this?"

"Oh, my dear! What an innocent you are! He is the most disliked of all her courtiers. His manners are slovenly, to say the least. His horsemanship—well, awkward would be putting it kindly. But as Renard said, 'He is proud and poor and stubborn, but worst of all, spiteful.'"

He's Mean Queen Carrie in guy form! Rose thought. And suddenly all the nasty things Carrie had ever said stormed through her brain. *Myles, how can you sew? All you can do is push a button? . . . I don't exactly hate you, but if you were on fire and I had water, I'd drink it. . . . I hear your boyfriend wears diapers. . . . Our leetil amigo . . . Marisol!* It all rushed back to Rose. Every vile, hateful thing that Carrie had hurled at all the kids she bullied.

Jane had continued talking. "He is determined to do the queen's bidding, to the point that she will finally succumb to his proposals of marriage." Jane took a deep breath. "To that end he goes to Mass not just three times a day as required, but four or five. And of course that he checks that all others do as well. He takes only Catholics into his service. Those Catholics who never rejected the faith in the time of young Edward. . . ." Jane paused again. Her painted lips began to quiver. "There have been rumors already, but as I was listening to him under the queen's bed, I heard that he suspects Elizabeth of not going to Mass. He of course has spies at Hatfield. There will be arrests made there and other places, especially in London, where groups of Protestants are said to hold secret services. There are clandestine groups of Protestants that meet throughout the countryside. There is even a book dealer in London who has been sent to the Tower for importing Bibles from Geneva."

"That's a crime now, isn't it?" Rose asked.

"Indeed."

"That's what I don't understand," Rose said. "Why is the Bible so bad?"

"The Bible was only translated from Latin into English thirty years ago. Then the common folk could read it."

"So what? Why isn't that good?"

"If they could read it, they could talk or argue about it. The pope would no longer have the last word. And the pope's power cannot not be questioned. Nor can Queen Mary's. She is set on destroying such questions. Edward Courtenay has presented her with a list of suspected Protestants. There are several in Princess Elizabeth's household."

Franny! Franny was a Protestant. When Rose had taught her to read, she said that the thing she most wanted was to save her wages to purchase a Bible.

"And the coals? What's that about, Jane?"

"They aren't just going to lock these people up in the

Tower. They will burn them at the stake."

"And he's whispering all this into the queen's ear?" Rose asked.

Jane nodded. "Rough wooing, I would say." Then Jane gave a harsh laugh. "I must be off."

Rose sat down hard on the steps leading up to the tower. Her father had warned her, after all. She was absolutely dizzy with fear, with shock. She shut her eyes tight and tried to banish the image of Franny being tied to a stake. The kindling bursting into flames. Then another image came into her mind—the smugglers, the ones they called coyotes, circling Marisol. And the Immigration and Customs Enforcement officers that Sam Gold had told them about. Until Marisol got her papers, she was endangered. If the agents grabbed her, she'd be off to a detention center. Rose had never felt so torn in her life. She needed to be in two places at once. At her grandmother's house in the twenty-first century, where she could help Marisol, and Hatfield, where she could warn Franny. And then there was her dad too—was he in danger already? "Oh, Dad," she sighed.

She touched that spot where the locket had hung. She almost felt nauseous when she thought of it hanging from Queen Mary's neck. If the queen opened it and saw the pictures inside, it would be over for Rose. It would be called witchcraft. *They burn witches here, don't they?*

Chapter 17

Without Darkness There Is No Light

Then she was back—back in her robe, wearing her fuzzy slippers. Indeed, she was in the very spot she had been when she had left. Standing in front of the graftling of the damask rose. She tipped her head to one side to study it more carefully. Was it drooping slightly? There was something more fragile about it. An uneasiness crept through her. How could it have changed so quickly? She must have only been gone a minute or two. That was the usual duration of her time travels. What might seem like months or years back in the time of the Tudors, the sixteenth century, might only amount to minutes or even seconds in her home century. She had not brought her iPhone down with her, but she recalled that it had been 12:01 when she tiptoed down from her bedroom—12:01 on the longest night and shortest day of the year. But there was no clock in the greenhouse. The nearest clock was in the library, where she, her gran, and Marisol had gathered hours before.

So she headed for the library. It was a beautiful room, and yet quite the opposite of the greenhouse. It was a place of darkness and shadows. She turned the switch and the soft amber glow of lights hung like halos in the walnut-paneled room. The scents of this room swirled around her. Scents of wood, leather, and the oil that was applied twice a year to the old leather-bound volumes. And also the fragrance of balsam from the Christmas tree.

All these smells were so different from that of the greenhouse, which seemed to be filled with the fragrance of life and growth. These odors certainly were not of death but of preservation. Many of the books on the shelves were old ones, rare and probably forgotten by most of the people on earth. There were histories and ancient encyclopedias. Also something her gran called Books of Hours, which were very valuable. They were tiny prayer books beautifully illustrated by monks in the Middle Ages. "I know," Gran had said. "You can google all this stuff. But I would rather have the weight of this leather volume number eight, with its lovely green spine and gold-embossed title, than one of those laptop things."

There were a few faintly glowing coals in the grate of the fireplace, and on the elaborately carved mantelpiece was an equally elaborate clock. The minute hand on the clock showed ten minutes past midnight. Rose blinked. She had never stayed so long in that other world. If she calculated the time it took her to go from her bedroom at 12:01 in the morning down to the greenhouse, it would have been no more than three minutes. Had she actually been at Beaulieu Palace for six whole minutes? Why? Was it because it was the longest night of the year? Did the time gods, or whatever it was that caused these tangled time journeys, grant her a few extra minutes because of the winter solstice? After all, it was a pretty complicated situation. A critically ill queen, her princely fiancé forced to cancel his visit. Then this total creep Edward Courtenay trying to court her by whispering disgusting things about burning innocent people.

Rose needed to think. She decided to turn on the Christmas tree lights. The moment they flickered on, she heard a soft meow. "September!" she exclaimed. The cat was by the Christmas tree and looking at the glittering silver ornament hanging from a low branch. Rose remembered how her cat back in Philadelphia would harass the Christmas tree until finally her mother had to hang the tree from a hook she installed in the ceiling.

"Oh, please don't bat it, September!"

September turned her head toward Rose. The limpid green eyes narrowed with the most scornful expression. As if to say *How could you even think such a thing!* Then the cat jumped onto the velvet sofa across from the fireplace.

Rose sat down next to September, who tucked in beside her. It was a bit chilly, so Rose pulled up the furry lap rug that her gran used to keep herself warm.

"Does this offend you?" she asked September. Apparently not, as September burrowed her nose into it. She began purring; it was the most endearing sound that a cat could make. It was as soothing for Rose as it was for September. She had once read that a cat's purr rate or frequency vibration was twenty-five hertz, or cycles, per second. Studies had shown that it could even promote healing. Rose yawned. She did feel as if she were healing in some way from the ugliness she had seen in the queen's bedchamber. The basins of blood. The fragile smile that twitched at the corners of Mary's mouth. It made her look truly nasty, especially with the treacherous Courtenay whispering in her ear. She yawned again. But something more niggled at the back of her mind. *Franny . . . I must help Franny.* She was so tired. Six minutes in the year 1553 was utterly exhausting. Well, of course. She must have been there for at least a month. After all, the dress was almost completed. She yawned one last time and fell sound asleep.

A bright blade of morning light slashed through the heavy draperies. She glanced at the clock. Eight o'clock! She got up and left the library. The house was unusually quiet for this hour. No sounds of Shirley the cook stirring in the kitchen or Calvin outside shoveling the walk. *Must be the solstice*, Rose thought. The longest night must have kept people in bed. She climbed the staircase and tried to be as quiet as possible so she wouldn't wake Marisol up.

But Marisol was down on her knees at the end of the bed. She appeared to be praying. When she looked up, Rose could see that she had been crying.

"Marisol, you all right?"

She sniffed and pressed something to her chest. "My mother's birthday. Light vanishing day."

"You mean the solstice?"

Marisol nodded silently. "*Solsticio*," she whispered.

"But it's not really that at all. You've got it confused—every day from now on will be longer and the darkness shorter."

"Here it's that way," Marisol said.

"Here?" Rose was slightly bewildered. Then it dawned on her. Marisol did not come from "here." She came from Bolivia, in the southern hemisphere, where it was just the reverse. At this time of the year, the days would be growing shorter and shorter.

"But . . ." And now there was the trace of a smile across Marisol's face. "My mother's name is Luz, for sunlight!"

Marisol got up and sat beside Rose. "See." She held out a tattered picture of her mother, Luz.

"She's beautiful, Marisol. You look so much like her." She could almost feel the lump growing in Marisol's throat as she fought not to cry.

"You know something?" Marisol said suddenly.

"What's that?"

"My birthday is exactly six months later, June twenty-first, where it is the winter solstice. In my country the days grow shorter and shorter now."

"And . . ." Rose paused.

"And what?" Marisol asked.

"Without the darkness there is not light to see."

A fleeting smile broke across Marisol's face. But then her brow puckered. "But . . . will I find her?"

Rose felt something collapse inside herself. "Will I find him?" she whispered. She hadn't meant to say it out loud.

"Him? Who are you talking about?" Marisol asked.

"My father." Her voice seemed to break.

"I thought you didn't have a father or a mother."

"It's hard to explain. I think . . . I think I have a father somewhere."

"Like me. I think my mother is somewhere out there too. . . ."

Her conversation with Marisol haunted her all day, and the idea of celebrating Christmas with her father continued to grow in Rose's mind. The problem was that every time she went back, she never knew what day or month she might arrive on. It had been early November last time. Who knew what month or year it could be, but what if somehow it were Christmas and she could celebrate it with her father and Franny? What gifts might she give them? She certainly knew that she had to get to Hatfield soon, to warn Franny about the growing danger to Protestants.

She turned to Marisol. "If you could give your mother a Christmas gift, what would you give her?"

"Oh, I already know. I almost have it made."

"Made?"

"Yes."

Marisol reached for the backpack she had been carrying to school on the day Rose found her in the snow. She took out a small, flat box tied with a red ribbon. She untied the ribbon and carefully began taking out sheets of paper. On each piece of paper there was a watercolor and colored pencil drawing. "Mama likes flowers, like your grandmother. I've been painting them ever since I came to Lincoln School. Ms. Adams, the art teacher, is so nice. I'm going to make some pictures for your grandmother too. I want to go down to the greenhouse and paint some of those beautiful roses."

"These are beautiful," Rose said as she leafed through the stack of drawings. "That's thoughtful of you, Marisol. It will mean a lot to my grandmother, I'm sure."

"She's a special lady, your grandmother."

They were not all flowers. Some were faces. "Who is this?"

"Guadalupe—a girl I met when I was riding the trains from Bolivia north. Very nice girl. Protected me."

There was a flinch of fear deep inside Rose. She dared not ask what Guadalupe had protected her from. There were close to thirty pictures. Some of people, some of flowers, some of sunsets and sunrises.

"You're really good," Rose said.

"You are too. I saw those bow ties you sold. Too expensive for me."

"I'll make you one for Christmas!"

"Aaah, that's nice."

Rose decided right then that she would also make her dad a bow tie for Christmas should they ever celebrate together. He'd be about two centuries ahead of his time, but let him be a trendsetter. Now, what might she make for Franny? Franny was always complaining about the coarse, scratchy hemp cloth she wore. Five hundred years ago there were stupid laws in England that ruled how people could dress. If you were a common person, a servant, you were not permitted to wear satins or velvets or brocades. Even certain colors were forbidden, like purple—strictly reserved for royalty.

But why not make Franny some pantaloons in velvet? No one would know, after all. This was underwear. There was even a new fabric she had found called Veltru that was a polyester synthetic velvet. It was so soft. Dared she make pantaloons in purple for Franny? No, better not chance it. She'd make them in gray—nice dull gray. The point was that the material would be soft. Softer than any of that scratchy cloth. Franny might as well be wearing a burlap bag for underwear.

All the rest of the day Rose and Marisol worked on their projects. Rose felt a bow tie wasn't really enough. She decided to make a whole new outfit for Marisol to wear to Christmas dinner. Susan and her mom and dad and older sister were coming. They always dressed up for things. Even though they were Jewish, they still sang carols and oohed and ahhed over Christmas trees. At least that was what Susan said. This was Rose's first Christmas with her gran. She had to get to work. Her first stop was to scroll back in her blog to an entry that was from much earlier. In her blog, she had a section called "Seeds." Things that inspired her, out of which other things grew. There was a dress that the famous painter Georgia O'Keeffe had worn, that was part of an exhibit along with her paintings. Rose absolutely adored that dress.

There it was! "Awww . . ." She sighed happily as she looked at the stunning picture of the white-and-black dress from the exhibit. The show was called Art, Image, Style. In Rose's mind, Georgia O'Keeffe and Frida Kahlo were the two most stylish artists ever.

Some Artist

Like "Some Pig!," the message Charlotte the spider wrote in her web for Wilbur in Charlotte's Web, *I would like to say "some artist" about my favorite style icon. Here's what was written about Georgia O'Keeffe in her high school yearbook:* A girl who would be different in habit, style and dress. *So, dear readers, when I first saw those words, I thought, here's my hero. Please note I did not say heroine. There are certain behaviors that are completely gender free. Like painter—sounds stupid to say paintress. We all own these words.*

Now Rose scrolled to earlier posts. The ones of Frida Kahlo.

Exhibit A: The Real Deal

Exhibit B: Me

Rose blinked at the picture and gasped. It was her, all right. On August 14, the day before her mom's fatal car accident!

"Are you all right?"

"Sure."

Rose looked up into Marisol's deep brown eyes. She saw not simply concern but anxiety.

She had been so determined to wipe out those days around the time of her mom's death. She had almost torn out the pages in the diary her mom had given her for her birthday. It was the last gift her mother would ever give her. She had studiously avoided looking back on anything before that terrible date. But now she had done it. Gone back to her own blog to the day before the crash. She felt a strange and unexpected calm begin to steal through her. Did this mean she was okay? Did it mean that she loved her mother less if she could so easily go back to this date now?

It was as if a scab had finally formed over a deep cut. She took a breath and gave a frail smile. "I'm fine, Marisol. I just have to get going on some presents myself. You've got a head start on me."

"You going to sew something? You sew so beautifully. . . ." She looked at Rose thoughtfully and smiled.

"You just wait and see, Marisol," Rose said slyly.

"You've got style, Rose. Real stylish girl." The soft Spanish inflection was like lovely music.

That morning Santa's workshop was officially opened in Rose's bedroom. Bolts of fabric were taken from the closet where Rose had neatly stored them. In the meantime, Marisol had gone down to the greenhouse and begun a series of greenhouse watercolors for Rosalinda. When Marisol ran out of paper and other art stuff, Calvin drove her to the art supply store. "Can you get me some colorful crepe paper while you're there?" Rose called out as they were about to leave.

"Crepe what?"

"Just ask the salesperson for paper to make artificial flowers."

"Artificial? What for?" Marisol asked. "There are real ones in the greenhouse."

"You'll see." She felt something flinch deep inside her. *Dad, I'll be back for you!*

Chapter 18

The Snow Fairy's Bat Mitzvah

"*And folks, it looks like another storm is coming our way. Is it a* snowmaggedon?" The weatherman's voice sounded quite joyful. "A new polar vortex is forming in the Canadian Rockies and sweeping down across the Great Lakes. It will be blizzard conditions by early this evening. They're calling this one 'Graymore.'"

"Graymore? Since when do they name blizzards?" Rose asked. But at that moment she wondered what her dad would think of naming blizzards. It was kind of weird, some of the things he didn't know—like the expression "stuck up." She'd thought that had been around for centuries. But they were all minor things that he didn't know. She could get him up to speed on everything he really needed to know. Well, not driving a car. But Calvin could teach him that. Oh jeez, could they have fun buzzing around in Gran's Bentley! Face it, she thought—she'd have fun chugging along in a jalopy as long as she was with her dad.

"Maybe blizzards got jealous of hurricanes and wanted names too," Marisol said.

Rose looked up from her sewing machine and laughed. "You're funny, Marisol." It delighted Rose that she was almost finished with Marisol's dress and Marisol still had no idea what she was working on. She'd whizzed through this dress. Of course it could not compare with the complications of sewing Queen Mary's meet-the-prince dress. No sewing machine and all those pearls to sew on! The dress had heavy brocade fabric, insets of lace, and five pounds of pearl trim—it was a heap of gaudiness, a complete fashion catastrophe. The Las Vegas of sixteenth-century gowns. And if the queen ever recovered and met the prince (which she would, as Rose had googled her death date—Mary died in 1558, so she had another five years to go) she would wear that dress. The question wasn't whether Mary would survive, but whether Rose would make it back to 1558. She had to! She had to get her father here. She had to warn Franny. Once again Rose felt as if she were being torn between two worlds—torn in half.

Just at that moment, they heard footsteps on the stairs

and Susan came into the room.

"Wow! This does look like Santa's workshop. What are you two elves up to?"

"Susan!" Both Rose and Marisol gasped. It was as if some snow fairy had alit in the bedroom.

"What? Oh yeah, I'm not wearing my glasses. I got contact lenses."

"It's not that!" Susan's hair was a jet-black froth of dense frizz. It flared out from her head like a halo. Her dark cloud of hair was luminous with sprinkles of snowflakes snagged midflight.

"Look at yourself in the mirror," Rose said.

"And your eyelashes are so long, and they have snowflakes in them too . . . they . . . they sparkle. You have snow lashes!" Marisol's voice was full of wonder.

"Well, I guess that's thanks to Graymore. By the way, they aren't just calling Graymore a blizzard. He will be a 'snow bomb' by tomorrow morning."

"What?" Rose said. "That's the stupidest thing ever. What's a snow bomb?"

"It's a kind of snow cyclone."

"Fine. But hold it right here before you melt." Rose jumped up and reached for her iPhone. "I need to get a picture of your eyelashes."

"And what about my nails?"

"¡Fantastico!" Marisol exclaimed.

"This is worthy of Instagram and my blog." Rose sat down. Her thumbs were flying as she posted the picture.

JEWISH CHRISTMAS ANGEL SIGHTING

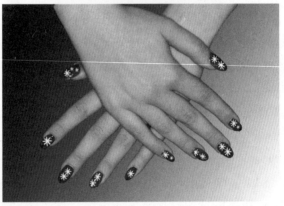

"I brought the nail polish. I can give you both manicures. I have all the stuff. The glitter and the teensy paintbrushes. I've been practicing."

"This is so cool," Rose said while Susan set up her

manicure space on a small table. "Here, have a gummy worm. New flavor for the holidays. Cranberry." Rose set out a package on the table alongside the manicure stuff.

"Oooh, yum. It's been months since I could eat a gummy anything. But I got my braces off too this week!" Susan replied. She grinned and batted her eyelashes, which had been hidden behind her glasses since she was six years old. "So, what design do you want?" She showed them some pictures from the manicure kit.

"I like the candy cane one," Marisol said.

"Oh good. That's pretty easy."

Fifteen minutes later Marisol held out her hands with her striped nails. "This is so nice. I want to try painting yours, Rose. You choose a pattern."

Rose looked at the various styles shown on the small piece of paper that came with the kit.

"Ooh, that's neat—the star of Bethlehem one."

"That's going to be hard," Susan said.

"Can I try?" Marisol asked.

"Okay, here's the tiniest brush in the kit."

"That's good, but I'm going to need a pin. Rose, can you get me one of your straight pins from sewing?"

"Sure."

Marisol began painting Rose's nails. Ten minutes later she had almost completed one hand.

"Wow, you're really good, Marisol," Susan said.

"She's great." Rose looked up. "If you think this is good, Susan, you should see her watercolors."

"Using the pin works perfectly for the snowflakes around the star," Susan said.

"*Sí*, I mean, yes. And look how the star moves from east to west on each nail. Very correct. Right?"

"Right," Rose and Susan both replied.

"Maybe I do your grandmother's. You think she'd like it?"

"I'm sure," Rose said.

"I'll leave the kit with you," Susan offered.

"*Gracias*. I mean, thank you."

Sappy Christmas music began oozing from the radio. "Have yourself a merry little Christmas . . ." Rose and Marisol both exchanged looks of sheer horror. This was the song that had kept blasting from the mechanical snowman when Rose had found Marisol half frozen on the sidewalk.

"We CANNOT listen to that song!" Rose shouted.

Susan whipped out her phone and hit the Music app. Naturally it was BYB, Boyz Will Be Boyz.

What's a boy to do? I miss you, I want to kiss you. I can't hear the beat without you, I can't feel the song . . . it's all so wrong. So wrong without you . . . girl. A dreamy look had swept across Susan's face.

"OMG, I forgot to tell you!" Susan's eyes were blinking rapidly. *Blinking beauty*, Rose thought. For there were still a couple of drops of melted snowflake water caught in Susan's long lashes.

"What?"

"Yuu Park."

"Who's Yuu Park?" Marisol asked.

"The lead singer of BWB," Rose answered. "Susan has a huge crush on him."

"He might be part Jewish!" Susan exclaimed.

"What? He's Korean. How can he be part Jewish?"

"I found out that his mom's name is Beatrice Silverman."

"So?" said Marisol.

"Silverman is a Jewish name. Have you ever met a Silverman who wasn't Jewish?"

"I'm not sure if I've ever met someone named Silverman," Rose said.

"Me neither." Marisol shook her head.

"But don't you understand? Being Jewish comes down through the mother. Fathers who aren't Jewish—that doesn't matter. It all comes through the mother. So Bea is probably Jewish."

"You're already calling her Bea?" Rose said. "And what's the point if he is Jewish or not?"

"The point is, maybe he could sing at my bat mitzvah? I mean, you know, maybe he'd sing for me. Since he's Jewish too."

"Well, maybe," Rose said.

"I think I'm going to write Bea."

"Okay." Rose and Marisol both nodded.

"And oh, I was also thinking of what to wear to your Christmas dinner. I'm thinking of my bat mitzvah skirt, the one that you cut down from the dress I bought at Old Souls vintage. Because I have two blouses now to go with it. You saw one but not the other, and I can't decide."

"I'll help you. Bring them both over."

"Just one problem."

"What's that?"

"Do you think it's appropriate that I wear a bat mitzvah outfit for Christmas dinner?"

"Don't be ridiculous. It's universal. You know—kind of ecumenical." And then a second later, Rose shouted, "Bonus points!"

"Oh yeah, 'ecumenical' was on the word list Mr. Ross gave us."

"Word list?" Marisol asked, perplexed.

"Oh, Mr. Ross sent it out on email that last day we had school," Susan said. "You didn't get it?"

"I . . . I don't have a computer."

"Jeez, that's . . . that's something," Susan murmured.

Marisol just shrugged. "More important things. You think, Susan, your dad is getting those papers for me?"

"Oh yeah, definitely. He's trying to speed things up. My

dad's real good at that kind of stuff. He can do just about anything."

My dad's real good at that kind of stuff. He can do just about anything. The words lingered in Rose's head.

Chapter 19

The
Gift

He can do just about anything. *The words still lingered in her mind* the next morning, Christmas Eve. Rose yearned more than ever to see her father. She wanted to give him a gift, a special gift. She had the bow tie, but that just didn't seem special enough. She had thought of making a very small album with pictures of herself and her mom. But that would be too dangerous. Not with Queen Mary wearing that locket on a chain around her neck. Nevertheless, Rose wanted to bring her dad some sort of Christmas gift when she went back. But who knew if it would be Christmas? The century was always the same—but the day, the month, the hour was anybody's guess.

Rose then suddenly remembered her mom's favorite

sweater. It was cashmere, with a timeless design of flowers entangled on a rich brown background. Obviously too small for her dad. But could she turn it into something else? She went to her closet and took the sweater off the hanger. Pressing it against her cheek, she was overwhelmed with a smell, a scent that was uniquely her mom's. There were layers of scent. First, there were the lilies of the valley that grew in the backyard of their house outside Philadelphia. And then she smelled the fragrance of a pasture dotted with wildflowers where they used to fly their kites. This was mingled with the salty breeze of the beach and the tang of sunblock. Then another scent—the velvet petals of roses, damask roses. All these scents flowed through her. She buried her face in the sweater. Like souls of something lost, they came back to her. But then she had a terrible thought. What if cashmere violated the sumptuary laws that governed what people could wear? What if cashmere was outlawed? Her dad could be arrested. Had cashmere been invented by the sixteenth century? She raced to her computer and googled it. Her heart sank when she read on Wikipedia that cashmere had been produced thousands of years ago in Mongolia, India, and Kashmir (naturally). Had anybody over four centuries ago known about those places? Marco Polo, the explorer, might have. Princess Elizabeth was very smart. She read history all the time. However, she had never mentioned Marco Polo. Two seconds later Rose

Marisol excused herself and went upstairs to finish her Christmas wrapping. Rose and her grandmother sat on the couch across from the fireplace. As Marisol left, Rosalinda's eyes followed her.

"Now, what's her name again?"

"Marisol, Gran." Rose suppressed a sigh. It was always so sad when her grandmother experienced these brief lapses.

"Oh, silly me. Why can't I remember her name?"

When Rose first came to live with her, Rosalinda would often turn to Betty and ask, "Now, who's that strange girl? What's her name?" Rose supposed it would continue. Her grandmother's memory was a bit frayed.

"I feel for her. She must miss her mother, especially tonight."

"I miss mine too," Rose said. "And my dad." It just slipped out. She hadn't meant to say it.

"Oh, dear girl!" Her gran gave her a squeeze.

A sob burst inside Rose. She dropped her head onto her grandmother's shoulder and began to cry. Rosalinda patted her and softly said, "There . . . there." The sound of her gran's words was in a sense like a cat purring.

Rose had never really mentioned her father, except once. She had asked Gran if she had known her father, and Rosalinda said no. But then her gran admitted that he might have come from "that time." "That time" was what her grandmother called those long-ago centuries where

Rosalinda herself had once gone. Rose now lifted her head and sniffled.

"You see, Gran, I actually met my dad."

"Really? You finally met him?"

Rose nodded and wiped her nose on her sleeve.

"And what is his name?"

"Nicholas Oliver."

"Ah, the goldsmith."

"You know him?"

"No, but his father was the court goldsmith before him, and everyone said that Nicholas would even exceed his father, William, in his talents."

"Well, I made a Christmas present for my dad."

"Lovely, dear. So why don't you go give it to him?"

"Really?"

"Of course. Why not go now?" There was a sly twinkle in her eye. "I'm sure you'll be back in time for Christmas dinner."

At that moment the clock on the mantelpiece began striking nine.

"But it might not be Christmas there. You know you can't ever predict what month you'll land in."

"What difference does it make? A gift is a gift. He'll love it no matter what day it is—Christmas Smishmas. Just go and give a gift of love."

"You're right, Gran."

She gave her grandmother a kiss good night. "Merry Christmas, Gran. You're the best."

Rose ran upstairs to get her present. Marisol was on her knees again, whispering her prayers in Spanish. She looked up at Rose.

"Where are you going?"

"Be back in three."

"Three what?"

"Three minutes. That's all it will take."

"*Feliz Navidad*, Rose."

"*Gracias*, Marisol."

Chapter 20

A
Message

Rose stopped briefly at the graftling, with the present tucked under her arm. Had it perhaps grown a quarter of an inch? Rose bent down, drawing her face close the stem.

And then she was back! Still crouched down, then shoving the present under the mattress of her tiny room in Whitehall Palace. She heard a soft tap on her door.

"Yes?"

"It's just me, Sara." There was a pause. "With the latest news!" She had forgotten that she now had a room all of her own. A servant had left and not been replaced. So Sara had taken the empty room for now.

Rose rolled her eyes. Sara was absolutely obsessed with the queen's possible engagement to the Spanish prince.

"Yes, yes, come in. Do tell all." Rose feigned enthusiasm. There was the sound of the paper crinkling under her, and she began to cough to camouflage it. Sara opened the door and came in, her eyes gleaming.

"Well, do you want my personal opinion on the engagement?"

"Of course. Do you think I can just waltz up and ask the queen her opinion on the engagement?"

Sara burst out laughing, and actually slapped her knee. "Oh, Rose, you have the oddest way of putting things. Waltz? What is a waltz?"

"Oh, just an old country dance from West Ditch. But what is the gossip about the queen?"

"Well." Sara was a rather thin girl and appeared to almost swell up before Rose's eyes, ready to burst with gossip. "As you know, the lord chancellor has been working mightily on the marriage contract. Just before Christmas they almost had one with Felipe. Actually it seems that it's mostly Felipe's father they have to please. And of course they got so close to settling the contract, which would have made Felipe king of England, at least as long as Mary lived. But you'll recall the horrible violence, the rebellion led by Mr. Wyatt. The Protestants hated the idea of the queen marrying a Spanish prince who someday might be king."

"Yes, yes," Rose answered softly. She had read online

about the rebellion. It had led to many being locked up in the Tower and several beheadings.

"Well, nothing has been settled. Not at all. They are no closer than when the rebellion happened, and that was months ago. It's even worse. Prince Felipe's visit has been postponed again. Lord knows when they will ever meet. And the lovely dress for the meeting still hangs unworn in the wardrobe. But the queen is now consulting with Waldegrave about some gilded brocade she wants for the wedding dress."

"So they aren't close with the contract."

"Not at all. That's my point. Felipe's father, the king of Spain, wants support from our queen for his army. This is NOT ever going to happen. Yet the order has gone through for the wedding dress fabric. What's that expression you use sometimes about chickens?"

"Counting your chickens before they hatch?"

"Exactly. They are as far from a wedding contract as can be and yet she's planning her wedding dress! And the court goldsmith has been summoned."

"What?" It was as if an electrical current had flashed through Rose. She sat up straight. She heard a tiny crinkle of wrapping paper from under the mattress where the present was hidden.

"Yes, Nicholas Oliver."

"To do what?"

"Create medals, of course."

"For what?"

"To commemorate the occasion of her marriage. It's the custom, you know." She paused a moment. "Oh, maybe you don't, as you weren't here back in those days when her father, King Henry, kept getting married. They say it made Nicholas Oliver a rich man. Every wedding, or at least the last three, he was making medals and of course wedding rings. I was serving for the last two weddings. Anyhow, you see what I mean. Queen Mary is counting her chicks before they hatch."

"So, when might the goldsmith be coming?" Rose tried with all her might to ask this as casually as possible.

"Soon, I think. Tomorrow."

Tomorrow! Tomorrow! The word exploded silently in Rose's head. She shifted and heard another crackle of the wrapping paper.

Rose could hardly sleep that night. Then it seemed as if she had been asleep for all of two minutes when she heard a slightly scratchy sound. Oh, she hoped it wasn't mice. These old palaces had immense populations of rodents running around all over. Poor fools knew nothing about hygiene. Although they were quite good in hunting down large animals with their bows and arrows, they had not scaled down to anything quite as small as a mouse. She always had to shake out her French hood to rid it of mouse poop. There were some super-icky parts of Rose's life here, but if it meant she could reunite with her father, what was a little bit of mouse poop? She got out of bed to explore the source of the skittering and saw a paper had been slipped under her door. She picked it up, opened the door, and saw the shadow of her friend slide around a corner. Bettina was one of the few servants who could read and write.

Dawn. Privy garden by the lion statue. Destroy this note.

This was not the first time that Bettina had delivered a message to her from her father. He was arriving and wanted to meet with her! Rose ran to her window and pushed the shutter open. The moon had slid away, perhaps hours before. She wasn't sure. The blackness of the night was beginning to fray. In another hour or less it would be dawn. Rose heard the chimes of the courtyard clock marking the half hour. She'd go now.

She slipped into her "neathies," which was what servant girls called their undergarments, and put on her chemise, a kind of lightweight fabric dress, and finally her kirtle. She shook the mouse poop out of her hood and put it on, with all her hair tucked under. She took the present from its hiding place under her mattress. Then she grabbed a heavy shawl and wrapped it around her. The clattering rain had ceased, leaving a gauzy mist that hung over the palace grounds.

She exited the east tower of the palace's servants' wing into the laundry courtyard. Then she followed a path from the courtyard that took her between the tennis green and the tiltyard, both of which had not seen much use since King Henry had died. Neither Henry's late son, King Edward, nor the present queen were athletically inclined. Of course, females never tilted. Rose always thought this was too bad, as poking an opponent off a horse with a jousting stick looked like fun. She herself had become a very good rider since moving to her grandmother's. Her gran had leased a wonderful pony for her, Ivy. But she didn't like to think of Ivy getting hurt. Apparently King Henry had lost more than one horse in tilting matches.

The ground fog seemed to thicken as she reached the end of the path, clutching the present to her chest. Soon she could barely see her feet. She was overwhelmed by a strange sensation. It was as if she were dissolving into this mist a few inches at a time, beginning at her ankles. Maybe she was like the Cheshire cat in *Alice in Wonderland* who periodically faded away, leaving only its grin.

By the time she turned into the privy garden, the fog was swirling around her. Stone statues reared through the scarves of mist that streamed through the garden. But the garden had been neglected. Although it was mid-March here, it felt closer to winter, as if February had stuttered along, leaving plants and and shrubs leafless. Buds were shut tight and almost withered looking. There was not even a promise of blossoming. She had been in this garden before at this same time of year, after Henry VIII died, and it had not looked like this then—not at all. She stepped up close to a hedge called King's Fool. It was one of the earliest shrubs to bloom, with large blossoms as big as saucers. Normally the buds would be swollen and green with the hint of a burst of a deep pink blossom. But these bud cases were brittle, as if withering on the stem. Shriveled as they were, Rose detected a crackling stubbornness, an absolute refusal to bloom. Nature had gone on strike!

Ahead she saw the stone mane of the lion rippling in the windless night. There was a bench just across from it. She approached quietly, sat down, and watched the sky. A dawn vigil. She tried to calm herself, but her heart was racing. The sky was growing lighter. Had a layer of darkness been peeled away? Yes, she was sure a stream of palest pink was beginning to softly glow in the east.

Chapter 21

The Kindling

Nicholas Oliver *caught his breath as he rounded the corner and* glimpsed his daughter, Rose, her head turned east toward the breaking dawn. She was as still as one of the stone statues. She clutched some sort of package in her arms. It seemed a miracle to him. She had come back. He knew that other people in his century were not aware of her absence. It was one of the oddities of these twenty-first-century time travelers. When her mother, Rosemary, would be gone, it might seem like only a minute to him. However, when she returned, she often seemed surprised that it was another season. Rosemary might say, "Oh, it was spring when I was here, and now it's almost autumn," or "fall," as she called it.

"Really?" he would reply. "Honestly, it seems like it was no more than a few minutes since I last saw you." But then those few minutes began to grow longer, into hours, and then days, and finally months. And yet he was the only one at Richmond Palace who noticed. There Rosemary had served Anne Boleyn, and then later she had served at Hatfield, where Princess Elizabeth was taken as a baby. Finally when the weeks stretched into months and the months to years, Nicholas Oliver knew that his beloved Rosemary was gone for good. They had talked of her bringing Rose here, but had decided it was simply too dangerous. And too confusing for Rose. So they both agreed it could never happen. But then Rose had traveled here on her own. And now she was back again. She was here, despite his warning.

He stepped out into the fragile dawn light just as Rose looked up. She sprang to her feet and rushed into his arms as he crushed her to his chest.

"Oh, Rose! Oh, daughter!" Rose felt a thrill pass through her. It was as if something within her had become more complete. He looked at the package in her arms. "And what is that?"

"A present for you, Dad."

"What? A present? For what occasion?"

"Well, where I come from, it's Christmas . . . Christmas Eve, actually."

"How strange! It's the eighteenth day of March here.

But time does tangle, as your mum always said."

They walked together over to the bench. He looked at the package. "What strange paper. Quite lively. Who is that little fat man in the red suit?"

"Santa Claus."

"Who?"

"Well, I don't think he'll be invented until many centuries from now. But kind of like Saint Nicholas."

"Oh, you mean the Christian martyr from Greece. I was named for him."

"I guess," Rose said.

"I never imagined him so fat and jolly."

"Uh . . . it's sort of hard to explain. He brings presents. He comes down the chimney when everyone in the house is asleep and puts the presents under the Christmas tree."

"How peculiar. Now, how does he get on the roof?"

Rose took a deep breath. "Well, he lands there."

"Lands there?" A baffled expression was in her father's eyes.

"Prepare yourself, Dad. It gets more peculiar. He comes in a sleigh from the North Pole. The sleigh is full of presents and is pulled by reindeer." She paused. Her father's deep blue eyes had grown wide with wonder. "And there are eight of them," she added. "Eight reindeer—wanna know their names?" Her father nodded. "Dasher, Dancer, Prancer, Vixen, Comet, Cupid, Donner, and Blitzen. . . . But Dad, maybe you should open the present I brought you." *No rein-deer, no sleigh, just a mysterious greenhouse,* Rose thought as she watched him untie the ribbon. She almost held her breath when he began to pull at the Scotch tape.

"Interesting. Never seen this before," he whispered as he peeled off the tape and held it up in the air. Then he opened the paper, and there was the sound of a sharp inhalation of breath. He seemed to go rigid. *God, what have I done?* Rose thought as she saw the color drain from his face. He picked up the cashmere scarf. "Her!" he exclaimed. "Your mum's scent." He buried his face in the soft fabric, just as Rose had when she had pulled the sweater from her closet. Rose put her arm around her dad's shoulders.

"Yeah, I know. I . . . I felt the same way when I found it." He looked up at her and smiled. His smile was like a beam of sunshine in this frail dawn. "It had been a sweater of Mom's, but I repurposed it." He looked at her closely. "Repurpose—so it would be something you could wear—a muffler around your neck. Something to keep you warm. You told me once it gets very chilly in your workshop in Stoke-on-the-Wold, and I thought this could keep you warm."

"Triply warm," he replied with delight. "The muffler, the scent of your mother, and you—the thought of you making this for me and bringing it here." He gestured at the garden and his hand grazed another smaller shrub of the King's Fool.

Poor things, she thought. "These flowers look like they'll never bloom, and here it is almost spring."

"Nothing wants to grow here anymore." There was a note in her father's voice that frightened Rose. It was not so much a statement as a prophecy, a bad omen. She decided to change the subject.

"Did Mom ever bring things to you?"

"Yes, of course—the pictures of you. The ones in the locket and some other things. I mostly had to hide them away for fear of them being found."

"Did she ever have trouble bringing things from here?"

"I think it took her a while, but she seemed to have mastered both imports and exports." He smiled.

Good! Rose thought. Now she could talk to him about coming back with her. "Dad, remember when we first met in May, it was at Hampton Court Palace? Not long before young King Edward died."

"Of course, my dear. A day I shall never forget."

"Remember how I asked if you could come back with me?"

He nodded solemnly. "And how many times since then have you asked?" He said this very soberly.

"I guess almost every time." She saw his brow crinkle.

Fear began to squirm deep in her stomach. *Was he going to say no this time?*

"Rose . . ." He began to speak slowly. "One of the reasons I came here was to warn you."

"Warn me? But how did you know I was here?"

"I know you are stubborn like your mum. Things are getting very dangerous here." He looked toward the east, where the sun had climbed higher. "Just about now Princess Elizabeth is being brought by barge to the Tower of London." Rose gasped. It was all becoming true, too true. "The queen has ordered Elizabeth's arrest as part of the conspiracy in the Wyatt rebellion. They were accused of trying to overthrow the queen because of her possible marriage to Prince Felipe."

"B-b-b-but . . . b-b-but she had nothing to do with that. Mary's always been jealous of Elizabeth—her beauty, her . . . her smarts . . ." She saw her father blink at that. "I mean her intelligence. Why would she do that?"

"Because"—her father's voice had dropped to a whisper—"she is a vile and desperate woman. She is unhinged. She has sent out warrants for the arrests of several suspected Protestant enclaves, groups that practice their religion secretly. People who own Bibles. It is now a criminal offense to own a Bible."

"But I don't go to Protestant prayer meetings, or whatever you call them. Not here. I go to Mass three times a day, as is required. I mean, I just sort of pretend. But the queen will never know the difference."

"Maybe not. But I'm worried about your friend Franny."

"Franny! What's happened to Franny? I miss her so! I haven't seen her since . . ." She tried to think back. Had it been when young King Edward died? That had been eight months ago.

"Everyone on the princess's staff at Hatfield is suspect."

"But she was only a dairy maid."

"Everyone," her father said sternly. "She hasn't been arrested yet, but if a rumor got around that she was in one of these secret groups of heretics or had a Bible, it could be very bad for her."

But, thought Rose, *Franny doesn't know how to read*. Then a second later she remembered. How could she forget that she herself had taught Franny to read? But surely Franny wouldn't have enough money to purchase a Bible. She paused a moment as a horrid thought came to her. "Will they chop off these people's heads, like King Henry did to his foes?"

"No. As I said before, the queen will burn them. The stench will spread from these fires. The smoke will cling to the air for days as a reminder to the heretics who do not follow her faith. Queen Mary is just gathering the kindling. Soon the pyres will be built throughout England. Piles of straw will be set around stakes wrapped in oily cloths. When these stakes are touched by a torch, people will burn."

"Dad, you . . . we have to protect Franny."

"I shall try my best. You shouldn't be part of it. It's simply too dangerous. You must return to Indianapolis as quickly as possible."

Rose shut her eyes and shook her head. Was she about to have first argument with her dad? At school her friends were always having fights with their parents—over curfews, doing homework, getting piercings. But did her fight have to be on such a historic scale? Was her dad grounding her? Or rather, ungrounding her? He was forcing her to go back to her home century.

"You are not part of this, Rose. You are my only child. You must go back to your own time, your century, your grandmother."

Rose plunged her hand into a deep pocket of her kirtle and crossed her fingers.

"Sure, Dad." She had just told her first lie to her father. *No way am I going back for good.*

When she returned to her room, she saw Sara sitting on her bed, perfectly still, with cold, narrowed eyes. The eyes of a predator. Rose gasped.

"What are you doing here?"

"Might I ask you where have you been?"

"No. I asked you. Why are you here? This is my room. Yours is down the corridor now, or had you forgotten?"

"I heard a crinkling sound when I was here before. It sounded a bit like paper." Dread flooded through Rose.

"So?"

"So Bibles are made of paper."

"It was not a Bible. It was a gift."

"For whom?"

"That is my business and none of yours."

"Prove it was a gift."

"I don't have to prove anything to you, Sara."

"But you do." Her voice was laden with threat. "Say the catechism." The words came out of her thin-lipped mouth like bullets.

"I am not a parrot. I do not have to perform for you. I shall not cheapen God by such mockery. And yes, that is what it is when a vicious little bully like yourself makes such stupid demands. Shame! Shame on you, Sara! Now get out of my room!"

Sara seemed taken aback by this outburst. She got up and walked out as if in a trance.

Rose sank, shaking, onto the bed. Her father was right. The danger was great. Damn! Sara was every bit as evil as the Trio of Doom.

Chapter 22

Migrant in Time

"*Hi," Marisol said as Rose came through the bedroom door. She was still shaking.*

Rose glanced at the clock: 9:05 p.m. on Christmas Eve. There was the ping of a text message. It was Susan.

See you tomorrow. That was fun yesterday!

But then she saw an earlier text message from six minutes ago. It was from an unknown number. Rose felt something curdle in her stomach as she read it.

Feliz Navidad to you and your leetel amigo.

This had the fingerprints, or the claw marks, of the Trio of Doom. But she had blocked their numbers. They must be using someone else's phone. *OMG*, thought Rose—*bullies all over the place. Just back from that idiot Sara, and now this.*

"What's wrong, Rose? You look like a spirit walked over your grave," Marisol said.

"Oh, nothing," Rose said, attempting a smile. "I'm tired. Mind if I go to sleep? Don't worry, you can leave your light on."

"I have a favor to ask you," Marisol said.

"Sure."

"Could you give me the list of words from Mr. Ross? I'd like to study them."

"Sure, but on Christmas Eve you want to study the word list?"

"I got a lot of catching up to do, Rose. Many words to learn."

Rose stood up and printed out the word list. "Want my dictionary too, so you can look them up if you don't know them?"

"Oh yes, you are so kind, Rose. I never met anybody kinder." Marisol looked up with such trusting eyes. To think, only minutes before, Rose had been looking into Sara's cold eyes, that brimmed with suspicion, the eyes of a predator.

Rose got into her bed and pulled up the covers. She watched as Marisol began studying the words, her lips barely moving as she silently sounded them out. There was occasionally the little wispy sound of the thin paper of the dictionary pages being turned as she looked up the meaning of a word.

Marisol had finally closed the dictionary and quickly fallen asleep. But Rose couldn't sleep at all. She felt once again torn between two worlds, and now three people. Her dad, Rosalinda, and Marisol. If she went back to the sixteenth century for good, it might kill her grandmother. Then again, it might kill her. The episode with Sara had been truly unnerving. And now, since that weird text, she was really worried about Marisol. Undoubtedly the text was from Carrie or Lisa. Probably not Brianna, as they had clearly dumped her. What business was Marisol's legal status to them? But they would stoop to anything. *Look what they did to Joe*, she thought—*broke his ankle*. How would they break Marisol? A broken bone would be easy compared to a detention center. How had she gotten herself into this situation? It was almost too much for her. She began to cry, burying her face in her pillow. "Mom . . . mom . . . ," she whispered into the pillow. "Why, why did you have to die?" It was all her mom's fault. And then she cried even harder. How could she have blamed her mom for dying? *What kind of a girl does that?* In that moment it suddenly struck Rose that she and Marisol shared a curious bond. They were both migrants of sorts. She reached for her diary by her bed. Then she felt for the crack in the headboard where she had wedged the key. This diary was the last birthday present her mother had ever given her before that monstrous date, August 15, when her mom had died in the car crash. She glanced at the clock by her bed. It was almost one o'clock in the morning. Christmas morning—four months, one week, and three days since her mom had died. She had a headlamp that she often wore for reading in bed. She put it on and turned away from Marisol so as not to wake her. Unlocking the diary, she began to write.

Dear Diary—Guess what! I was just thinking about Marisol and suddenly I have this weird, bizarre thought. Marisol and I share something. Marisol is a migrant of place and I am a migrant in time. That is sort of astounding. She's worried about getting caught and sent to a detention center, and I worry about being caught and burned at the stake. Dad's really worried about Franny and me. She's my best friend in England—England of more than four hundred years ago. I know I'll have to go back—I have to help them. But not right now. It's Christmas. But when I do go back, Sara better not get in my way!

She shut the diary, locked it. Then fell sound asleep—
at last.

It was the scent of cinnamon that woke her.

"Ooooh!" Marisol said, sitting up in her bed, stretching, and sniffing the air. "*¿Qué es esto?* . . . I mean, what is this?"

"Shirley. She baked my favorite thing for breakfast—cinnamon sticky buns."

"Then we must go down to breakfast with *alacrity*!" Marisol giggled.

"Whoa, you really did learn those words!"

"I need words—lots of words," Marisol said cryptically. Her eyes hardened with a determined look.

They heard a soft knock.

"It's me, Betty."

"Oh, Betty, I nearly forgot." Rose leaped from her bed.

"Forgot what?" Marisol asked.

"I promised to help Gran get dressed. Because Betty is taking the day off." She opened the door.

Betty was standing there wearing a colorful puffy beret. It was a patchwork of different colored velvets. Rose had decorated the edges with quarter-inch gold braid trim. She loved the soft hats that so many of the men wore back in the sixteenth century—including her father. They of course didn't call them hats, but bonnets. Often they had feathers attached and were decorated with jewels as well, if the man was wealthy. Men would never think of wearing such hats now, in her home century, but back then men were much more daring. She had seen Henry VIII only once before he died. But he certainly wore a bonnet with a great deal of style. His were trimmed in ermines and sometimes dripping with pearls—the go-to gem for clothing.

"Don't worry, dear," Betty said. "She's up and dressed for breakfast, but maybe you can help her downstairs. I've laid out her clothes for Christmas dinner."

"Oh, thank you, Betty."

"You're welcome, dear. I'll be back by this evening to get your grandmother ready for bed." She started to leave, then touched her hat. "Oh, I nearly forgot to thank you for the nice velvet hat you made me. So stylish, yet warm and cozy. A hat of many colors. And with my painted nails— thanks to you, Marisol—I'll be quite the belle of the ball at my niece's house." She gave a wave and ducked out of Rose's room.

"We'd better go down and put our presents under the tree. Gran says we'll open them after breakfast."

Gran insisted that Shirley the cook sit down with them for breakfast.

"No one should have to work on Christmas Day, Cook. Please take a seat." Rose always winced a bit when her grandmother called Shirley "Cook." Of course, Cook, coincidentally, was Shirley's last name. But it sounded slightly rude to Rose, even though she knew that her grandmother never intended it to be. "And I expect you to sit with us at Christmas dinner as well."

When they were all seated in the conservatory, the damask roses they had moved from the greenhouse a short while ago were all in beautiful full bloom, with more buds about to open. In hanging pots there were also spring bulbs—hyacinths and some miniature daffodils. On a trellis between the windows, pale lavender clematis had opened. Rosalinda looked about the beautiful room. She seemed to be registering every blossom of every flower.

"Gran, look, the clematis that I brought out just two days ago opened."

"Indeed. I told you so."

"I didn't believe you. We had a bet. I owe you a dollar."

"Yes, you do!" She laughed.

"This is so beautiful, Mrs. Ashley," said Marisol.

"I told you, dear, just call me Rosalinda. Remember, we're almost relatives now."

"Almost," Marisol said wistfully, as if she didn't quite believe that what she wanted to happen most in the whole world, next to finding her mom, could happen. Rosalinda seemed to read her mind. She patted Marisol's hand.

"You see, here we sit with flowers blooming in the winter that usually don't bloom until spring, or summer." She nodded at the clematis vine that was laden with blossoms.

"The seasons are tangled here. Summer roses in December, side by side with spring tulips over there." She pointed with a gnarled finger to the pots of miniature tulips as Shirley brought in a fresh basket of sticky buns. There was not only a tangle of seasons in the room, but a tapestry of heady fragrances being woven around them. There was the drowsy sweetness of the cinnamon sticky buns and the spicy tang of a flowering ginger plant. The perfume of the roses mingled with the earthy scent of the spring bulbs. They all seemed to become part of this lovely tapestry that her gran had woven. She was, Rose thought, a weaver of time and seasons. Rosalinda was an artist.

They all went into the library to open their presents. Rose insisted that Marisol open hers first. She watched as Marisol so carefully untied the ribbon and then layer by layer removed the tissue paper. It was almost as if she had never opened a gift before. There was something sad about the care she took. It was as though she thought she might break the gift, or perhaps that it would just vanish into thin air.

But when she removed the last piece of tissue paper, Marisol caught her breath.

"What is it?"

"A dress. A dress for Christmas dinner," Rose said.

Marisol picked it up and held it in front of her. Her eyes

were shining. "It's so beautiful—the black, the white. It . . . it reminds me of a . . . a swan, a swan with black wings."

"It's a copy of a dress worn by a great artist, Georgia O'Keeffe. And just for a touch of color I made you this." Rose held out a glittery pink gift bag.

"What is it?"

"Open it!"

Marisol drew out a ring of bright crepe paper flowers. Her eyes grew wide with delight.

"I made it . . . but was inspired by another artist. Frida Kahlo."

"But what is it for?"

"Your head. It's a headband. You can't be just all black and white. Not on Christmas."

Marisol ran up to Rose and embraced her. Rosalinda's eyes sparkled with tears.

There would be more tears as they opened the rest of the presents. Rosalinda was spellbound by Marisol's paintings of the greenhouse flowers. She called for her magnifying glass. "Look!" she exclaimed. "You even got the stamens and the pistils on the fairy lily." She put down the magnifying glass. "Marisol, dear, you could become a botanical illustrator. You could become the next Arabella Gilmore."

"Who?" Marisol asked.

"Most famous American botanical artist ever. She specialized in flowers of the rainforest."

Marisol clapped her hands. "There were rainforests near where I lived in Bolivia."

Then Rose opened Marisol's gift to her.

"Ivy!" she cried. Marisol had noticed the photograph of Rose's pony, Ivy, when she had first arrived. Rose had taken the picture on her iPhone, then posted it on Instagram. Her grandmother had insisted on having a large print made, which she had had framed and hung in the library. She had also made a smaller one for Rose to have on her desk.

"How did you do this? I mean, this isn't just a copy."

"No, I never just copy. It's a painting with acrylics. I haven't used acrylics very much, but Ms. Adams showed me how. I put some sunlight in the painting so you could see Ivy's eyes better. They are such beautiful eyes."

"Dreamy eyes, I always think," Rose said. It had been nearly two weeks since she had been at the riding academy because of all the snow. She couldn't wait to get back. As she looked at the picture of Ivy, she could almost feel the sensation of Ivy gathering her muscles as they approached a jump. Then that almost mystical moment when Ivy's hooves left the ground and together she and the pony sailed into thin air over the jump.

There were more presents, including a box of wonderful fabrics and hand-painted silks that Rosalinda had ordered from Thailand for Rose's future sewing projects. After they had finished opening their presents and oohing and aahing over the perfectness of each gift, a drowsiness began to envelop them.

"I think I'll need a nap before Christmas dinner," Rosalinda said.

Three hours later they all gathered again with Susan, her sister and father and mother, and Dr. Seeger for Christmas dinner. Rose looked at the guests. This, she realized, was her new reconstructed family. But there were still gaps, and some could never be filled in. "You only live once"—that was the saying. She thought of her mother. She thought of what a lovely couple her mother and her father would have made, in this world or that other one.

Should she go back now? Right now, just for a minute? Would anyone miss her? Her father's voice streamed through her mind. *Queen Mary is just gathering the kindling. Soon the pyres will be built throughout England. Piles of straw will be set around stakes wrapped in oily cloths. When these stakes are touched by a torch, people will burn.* And then she remembered Sara—those pale predatory eyes. The hateful conversation seeped into her brain. *Prove it was a gift. I don't have to prove anything to you, Sara. . . . But you do.*

She clutched her napkin and tried not to wince as Shirley brought in the dessert—a flaming Christmas pudding.

"And ice cream," Rosalinda said in a tinkly voice. "For those who do not like brandy-soaked cake."

"Ice cream!" Rose blurted out. It was a relief to think about ice cream. And not Sara or burnings.

A vague look filled her grandmother's eyes. She giggled and then in a soft singsongy voice began whispering to herself. "Ice cream, ice cream, we all scream for ice cream."

Uh-oh, Rose thought. This was always a sign that her gran was tired and growing slightly confused. Rosalinda leaned in close to Rose and whispered, "Who is that girl sitting across from me? What's her name?"

"Marisol, Gran. Remember, you're her sponsor," Rose whispered. Gran looked at Rose as the confusion welled up in her eyes. The question "sponsor for what?" went unasked.

The
Burning Queen

Chapter 23

Pugs
and Pixies

Word list for January 17:

Metaphor

Oxymoron

Imperil

Redundant

Anxiety

Supercilious

Sanctimonious

Arrogant

Embellish

Escalate

The new words were on the greenboard in homeroom. There was a crackling noise over the PA system.

"Good morning, students." It was Ms. Fuentes, the school principal. "Welcome to the second week of the new year. As you know, tonight is the high school campfire at Lake Marian for the city college scholarship fund. The ticket price is just one dollar for students from Lincoln Middle School, but no admission unless we have received the consent form from your parent or guardian."

Rose was sitting behind Carrie as she turned around. If there was anyone who ever looked like a pug dog, it was Carrie. Her mouth curled into an ugly smile. "'Parent' or 'guardian.' Hear that, *amigos*?"

"Put a plug in your pug mouth." Rose's voice seared the space between them. Carrie turned around and Lisa giggled. They high-fived each other.

"No talking in the back there, ladies . . . er, I mean girls." Mr. Ross stood up from his chair and pointed at all three of them.

On their way out of homeroom to their first class, Mr. Ross waved for Rose and Marisol to come up to his desk. Was she getting into trouble for talking? Rose wondered. But why Marisol? She hadn't said a word. Rose was tempted to tell Mr. Ross exactly why she had been talking to Carrie—a rare event indeed.

"Hello, Rose and Marisol. I was wondering if on break

after your math class you could meet me in the library. Don't look frightened, Marisol. It's all good. Just want to discuss something with you."

"Sure," Rose said as Marisol nodded.

There was the sound of something clattering to the floor at the back of the room.

"Oh, sorry, Mr. Ross. I guess I bumped that bookshelf," Lisa said.

"I've got to get maintenance in here to steady that. Don't worry about it."

"Thanks, Mr. Ross." Lisa tilted her head and gave Mr. Ross one of her hundred-watt smiles, enhanced by the sprinkling of glitter she sometimes wore on her eyelids.

Their next class was French with Ms. Stone, or Madame Pierre, as she insisted on being called. In French the word *pierre* meant "stone." Madame Pierre, however, was anything but a stone. Maybe a tiny pebble. She had curly white hair that fluffed up like a small cumulus cloud over her head. Everything about her was tiny. Super—rather—*très* petite. Her nose was pink like a rabbit's and ended in a roundish nubbin that seemed to be double-jointed. When she sniffed—as she often did—the nubbin took on a life of its own.

"*Bonjour, mes amis.*"

"Or *amigos*," Carrie said softly, and giggled.

What is it with her?! Rose thought. She immediately got up from her seat and moved away as far as she could.

"*Qu'est-ce que c'est, Mademoiselle Rose?*" Madame Pierre asked.

"Uh." Rose began to attempt to answer in French. That was what they were supposed to do. Rose's French was decent but not great. "*Je suis . . .*" Madame Pierre nodded encouragement. "*Je suis mal à,*" she began. "How do you say—I mean, *comment dit-on en français* 'uncomfortable'?"

"*Vous dites 'mal à l'aise.' Ca c'est l'idiotisme*, the expression for 'uncomfortable.'" Madame Pierrre replied, then said, "*Pourquoi êtes-vous mal à l'aise?*"

OMG—or oh mon Dieu, Rose thought. *This might go on forever.* What she would have liked to say in French was "I am uncomfortable because I'm sitting next to this total scumbag of a girl. This nasty, horrid, conniving, pathetic excuse for a human being." Luckily at that moment there was the crackle of the PA again, and Ms. Fuentes's voice came through. "Students, I neglected in my earlier announcement to tell you that those who want to sign up for spring soccer should get the forms from their homeroom teachers. Yes, I know spring seems a long time away. Thank you and have a good day."

Math followed French. As the class concluded, Marisol and Rose picked up their books and headed toward the library to meet with Mr. Ross, who was waiting for them at a table in the back corner.

"Marisol, I have heard the wonderful news about you finding a place in Rose's home and that Rose's grandmother is enthusiastically agreeing to sponsor you. I cannot express how wonderful I think this is—what your grandmother is doing by becoming a sponsor for Marisol. I understand that Susan Gold's father is helping out, and I wanted to assure you that I am available to help as well. I have talked to Mr. Gold about this. Ms. Fuentes too is aware of that, Marisol." He paused a moment. Rose had a weird sixth sense that someone was listening, eavesdropping. Then a few moments later she saw a shadow sliding by between the tall bookshelves. A topknot gave it away. Jenny the sixth grader! Darned if they hadn't recruited Tinker Bell. The conversation with Anand from just before Christmas came back to her. About who would replace Brianna in the Trio of Doom. Who would be the next Mean Queen? *Someone, I'm sure*, Rose had said. *Power vacuum*. Well, Tinker Bell had replaced Brianna.

"Excuse me just a minute," Rose said, getting out of the chair and going around the corner to the aisle between the bookshelves.

"Oh, hi, Jenny. Fancy meeting you here."

"Er . . . uh . . . just looking for a book about, uh . . . turtles."

"Turtles? Oh, they interest you?"

"Yes." She nodded rapidly. A sprinkling of tiny bits of glitter fell from her topknot.

"Really now, that's interesting." Jenny nodded again. More glitter. "Has someone written a biography of a turtle, or has a turtle written its autobiography?"

"Huh?" Jenny said.

"You're in the biography section, not natural science." Rose pulled a book from the shelf. "Here's a really good biography on Martin Luther King. I've read it. Twice, actually, and Martin Luther King Day was yesterday. Why don't you take this?"

"Yeah." Jenny reached for the book, avoiding Rose's eyes.

"And Jenny, if you're going to do the bidding of the Mean Queens, you really have to polish up on your spy skills."

Jenny grabbed the book and walked away as fast as she could.

Rose returned to the table. "Sorry. I just had to tell Jenny Rodgers something."

"Well," Mr. Ross said, "I was just telling Marisol that Ms. Fuentes herself was an immigrant from Guatemala when she was just about Marisol's age. So they have much in common. Ms. Fuentes is eager to help as well."

"Oh, that's really great!" Rose tried to express as much

enthusiasm as possible, but she was worried. The Trio of Doom had a new recruit—a pixie with a bent toward evil. Not just mischief. Teasing was mischief. Bullying was evil. Mischief was playful. Evil was deadly.

That evening was unusually warm. At the Lake Marian scholarship fund-raiser, the winter constellations climbed into the blackness of the moonless night. Below, a huge bonfire burned. *This is almost perfect*, Rose thought as she watched the tip of Orion's sword scrape over the horizon. She was sitting on a log next to Anand. Susan was on the other side next to Marisol. Next to Susan was Joe. She wondered if they were holding hands. She also saw that Anand sort-of-maybe-possibly had a crush on Marisol. Myles was in his wheelchair at the end of the log. They were all drinking hot chocolate. Some kids were out skating on the pond. Some were sledding. Some were building snow people. There was the scent of hot dogs cooking on the many grills that had been set up.

"Do you know why stars twinkle?" Myles asked.

"Nope," Joe said.

"Their light twinkles in a monochrome of pure silver chloride," Myles replied. "But actually there are colors to the stars. We just can't see them with our human eyes."

"Why?" Rose asked.

"Rods and cones," Myles said. "We have two kinds of

light receptors. Cones are color sensitive. Rods are color-blind but good in low light."

The leaping flames of the fire printed jagged shadows on the ground. Rose stared at the manic dance of the shadow flames. Then she glimpsed a wink of glitter in the night. A disco ball? No, of course not. Tinker Bell, in all her pixie dust glory. Rose gave a little gasp.

"What is it?" Susan said.

"Tinker Bell."

"What are you talking about?"

"Jenny."

"That sixth grader?"

"Yep. Remember the power vacuum? Jenny has filled it."

"Good grief, you're right. Look at them!" Carrie with her neon-blue hair streak, Lisa following, and then Jenny, all walking in single file. "She's a Lisa wannabe, isn't she?" Susan whispered.

"She's got her tiara of glitter but not quite a crown yet," Rose replied. "She's a princess-in-waiting for her place with the Mean Queens."

Rose stared into the flickering flames of the fire. There was something mesmerizing but tantalizingly dangerous about it. She felt herself succumbing to the thrall of this fire and yet almost paralyzed with fear. What would she do if Sara kept prying? What if she were tied to a stake at the center of fire and flames? She tore her eyes from the bonfire and looked out toward the lake. The ice was still solid. At least she hoped so, as Brianna was skating out there. She seemed carried by an invisible force. She lifted her right leg high into an arabesque and then continued to glide. The tip of that raised skate seemed to prick the sky. Then she lowered her leg and began skating very fast, then faster, at an almost unbelievable speed. Then she leaped into the air, still spinning around. Her hand reached out as if she were grabbing for a star. *Can you cut yourself on a star?* Rose wondered. She knew that she had never seen anything quite like what she had just witnessed. Was she the only one who had seen Brianna do this?

When they returned home that evening, the scent of the bonfire smoke seemed to have seeped into their clothes. It really began to bother Rose.

"Mind if I open a window to air out the smell of the smoke in our clothes?"

"Oh no, not at all." Marisol sighed.

"What's wrong?"

"I just worry—all the papers and things for me to be . . . safe, for your grandmother to become my sponsor, are taking so long."

"I think it was all that snow. A lot of city government offices were closed. And things, you know, get clogged."

"Clogged?"

"Plugged up, slowed down."

"I still am so scared. I saw a headline today in the newspaper. It said that more than one hundred thousand people from El Salvador were being sent back to their country."

Rose was quiet. She didn't know what to say. It would sound so lame to say "don't worry." Rose had an odd thought. If things didn't work out for Marisol, if the Immigration and Customs Enforcement officers came for her, the ICE men, Susan had called them, if they came right here to their front door at 4605 North Meridian Street, could Rose get her out? Could she actually tuck Marisol away in that past century, across the sea, in England? Or would that be like jumping from the frying pan into the fire? Another favorite expression of her mom's. It now sent chills up her spine. Marisol was Catholic. Calvin drove her to Mass on Sundays. She'd be fine in England. Safer than Franny. *Good grief*, Rose thought. *How did I end up with two IMPERILED friends?* Bonus points for using a word-list word. But peril seemed to swirl around her.

Anxiety seemed to hang in the air as thick as the scent of the bonfire. It soon became chilly in the room, so Rose closed the window.

"Night, Marisol."

"Night, Rosa. I mean, Rose."

"No problem. I like it when you call me Rosa. Night again." Somehow it seemed wrong to say "sweet dreams."

Chapter 24

The Dress

S he wasn't sure how long she had been asleep, but she felt something soft brush across her face. She opened her eyes. "September. What are you doing here? Where have you been? How did you get here?" September slitted her eyes and gave a small sniff as if to say, *Really? How did I get here?* Then the cat nodded toward the window and gave a deep purr— a SUPERCILIOUS purr, Rose thought. She obviously had not completely shut the window. September leaped lightly from the bed and onto the floor. Standing by the door, she tipped her head. It was clear now what September wanted. She wanted Rose to follow her to the greenhouse and go back, back to that other time—that kindling time, when the pyres were about to burn. Rose began to feel scared, but she knew she had to see her father again, and Franny. Rose scrambled out of bed and as quietly as possible put on her robe and fuzzy slippers. *Here we go again*, she thought. She glanced at her bedside clock. It was three minutes past one in the morning. She had a sudden thought. Why not take her iPhone? How cool would that be if she could somehow take some pictures? She had transported things back and forth over these borders of time—Jane the Bald's shoe to get it repaired. And then there was the acne cream for Princess Elizabeth, and of course several discarded ruffs. Sure, she could take her iPhone. No problem. She slipped it into the pocket of her bathrobe.

She stopped briefly at the damask rose graftling. "Oh dear!" she muttered. It looked slightly shriveled. She remembered her gran saying that roses were "heavy feeders." This one needed feeding. Potassium! She had helped her grandmother put the "lollipops," as her gran called the potassium sticks, in the other roses, but they weren't just seedlings or graftlings. They were full grown. She didn't want to overdose this one. She went to a shelf where the lollipops were kept in a box. September meowed.

"Just a minute, September. I have to take care of this graftling." She took out her iPhone from her bathrobe pocket and used the flashlight to read the instructions. *For seedlings use half a stick. All right*, she thought, setting down the phone. She went to the sink and wet the stick, which would release the potassium slowly. "Good luck," she murmured to the plant.

And then she was back. She was walking across the spreading lawn between the gatehouse and the palace of Beaulieu. It was a brilliant sunny day in May. She saw the shiny bald head of Jane the fool approaching.

"You should wear sunblock, Jane, or your head will be scorched." As soon as the words were out, Rose knew she'd made a serious error.

"Sunblock? Now that's a witch's brew if I've ever heard of one."

"Oh no. I meant to say a cap to block the sun. I can make you one."

"Out of those?" Jane asked nodding at the stack of material in Rose's arms.

"Probably not. These are swatches for the queen to choose from for her wedding dress. I guess it's all settled now, more or less."

"Well, so they say." Jane's right eyebrow scooted up to her domed bare scalp, indicating doubt rather than faith.

"You don't believe it, Jane?" Rose knew—how, she was unsure, but as soon as she walked out of the greenhouse into the palace grounds she had instant knowledge of the basic state of things. The marriage contract been signed after all. According to the announcement, it made Mary, through her marriage to Felipe, a ruler of many countries beyond England. She would be officially known as Mary, Queen of England, France, Naples, Jerusalem, and Ireland, Princess of Spain and Sicily, Archduchess of Austria, Duchess of Burgundy, and on and on. It seemed to Rose that it wasn't about love, but more about real estate. How romantic! Mom would have loved it, she thought. For Rose's mother had been one of Philadelphia's leading Realtors. What was that other thing her mom used to say—a rea estate quip: *It's all about location, location, location.* Well, it seemed to Rose that Queen Mary would have a minimum of about half a dozen countries to locate in. How would she ever cycle through all those palaces, much less the ten or more she had in England? Ridiculous!

It was at Beaulieu that the marriage plans had been set. The queen and Prince Felipe of Spain were to be united in holy matrimony on July 25 in Winchester Cathedral. Had the "happy couple" met yet? No, but that didn't seem to concern anyone. It was much more worrisome that the bridegroom-to-be had not sent one letter to his intended bride.

"No email?" Rose began to cough, attempting to disguise the word that had just slipped out. *Dear Lord*, she thought. *I have to get with the program.* "No letters yet to her from the prince?" Jane shook her head. The pulse in her bulging eye throbbed a bit, making it dance around. "Well, I do feel sorry for her." Rose sighed.

"Don't feel too sorry for her," Jane whispered hoarsely. Her eyes darted every which way, as if to catch a spy. "Of course the good news is that she let the princess out of the Tower. But she's still under arrest at Hatfield, and then they plan to take her to Woodstock."

"Woodstock? What's that?"

Jane looked surprised. "You don't know?" She paused a moment. "Oh, I always forget how young you are. Indeed, in all the time I've known you, Rose, you haven't aged a bit." This always made Rose quake, when people in the court mentioned her age or lack of aging. Jane herself had aged quite a bit. She had several wrinkles and didn't often turn cartwheels in court these days. Touch of gout, she had told Rose. Rose assumed that gout was something like arthritis, which often made the knuckles in her gran's fingers swell to the size of marbles.

"Woodstock is the old king's hunting lodge." Rose knew that when people said "old king," they were referring to Henry VIII. "And when the king wasn't hunting, he was wooing. He wooed Elizabeth's mother, Anne Boleyn, there, and Jane Seymour, the mother of little King Edward—God rest his soul."

"Hate to rush off, but I had better get these swatches to the queen. Is you-know-who there?" Rose asked, and Jane laughed.

"You mean she-who-must-not-be-named?"

Voldemort! It nearly slipped out. Rose almost bit her tongue. No way would Jane know about Voldemort. Harry Potter and J. K. Rowling would not be along for another five hundred years or so.

Jane smiled. "The one you call Snail Head?"

"Yes, indeed." So far Rose had also managed to avoid Sara—thank God! Sara was still back at Whitehall Place finishing up some sewing for the queen's ladies-in-waiting.

"Snail Head, or Lady Margaret, is there, but not in best favor. Not since Courtenay's arrest. It happened at the same time as Elizabeth's."

The queen had come around to suspecting that the man who was trying to woo her was possibly also involved in the Protestant rebellion.

A few minutes later Rose was passing through the presence room to be received in the queen's privy chamber.

"Oh, at last!" the queen exclaimed. "The swatches for my gown. How delightful." She waved her hand in the air, shooing away her councillors. "This is not men's business," she announced, turning to Jane Dormer and another lady-in-waiting, Susan Clarencieux. She had become especially close with Susan since her engagement. "Now let's see what you've got."

Rose curtsied and then began spreading out the pieces of fabric on a broad table from which the councillors had cleared their documents. They were truly the richest, most beautiful fabrics Rose had ever seen. In her home century, they might have cost hundreds of dollars a yard. But, of course, royalty didn't ask about prices. There was, however, not a single white fabric in the lot. Rose supposed that white was not in for wedding gowns. The queen stood close to the table, and because she was quite nearsighted, she bent over and squinted at the fabric. As she did, the rose pendant swung from her neck. A rage threatened to boil deep within Rose. She wanted to snatch the pendant from her neck. The queen, after flipping through two dozen or more pieces of fabric, straightened up. "I think this one." She casually wrapped the chain of the dangling locket around her finger. "What do you think, Lady Susan?" It was a plum-colored satin with an overlying intaglio design of leaves and flowers.

"And you?" She turned to Rose. "What do you think?" *Me, think?* "Can you work with this?"

"Yes, Your Majesty."

Jane Dormer stepped forward. "I would suggest, milady, that perhaps cone sleeves could be made with insets at the wrists in a contrasting color. Perhaps a pale silvery fabric."

"Excellent idea!" The queen clapped her rather pudgy hands together. She wore glittering rings on eight of her ten fingers. Her hands were in truth the only pudgy part of her. Quite in contrast to her scrawny neck, from which the locket hung.

"And a traditional ruff."

"Really?" Lady Susan asked.

"Yes, why not?" the queen replied. Her hand went to her neck. Was she aware of what an ugly neck she had? Rose wondered.

"It's so . . . so . . . so like your sister to wear a ruff." *So Elizabethan!* thought Rose. But did they use the term yet? A dark shadow crossed the queen's face. Her thin lips pursed. "Well, she doesn't own the style. Does she?"

"Of course not, ma'am." Lady Susan dipped into a minuscule curtsy.

"I could change it slightly and make a new kind of collar," Rose offered.

"You could?" the queen asked.

"Yes, Your Highness." Rose dipped into a slightly deeper curtsy.

"What would it look like?"

"I was thinking of a petal-style collar."

"Petal-style?" the queen asked.

Rose had seen the style on Etsy. "Well, imagine, if you will, flower petals, maybe even rose petals," she said, staring directly at the gold rose locket that her father had made for her mother. *I'm going to get that back . . . some way . . . somehow.* The queen's puffy fingers went to the locket.

"That seems appropriate. Yes. I like the idea."

"I'd make the petals larger, of course, and perhaps out of the same fabric as the wrist insets."

"Yes! Can you bring me a design? A sketch."

"Yes, Your Majesty." Rose curtsied again.

"Now, if we have decided on this as the main fabric, I feel that we should send out the samples of all the fabrics that will be in the dress with strict commands that no woman attending the wedding can wear anything close to the materials or the design of the wedding gown of the queen."

"Very sound suggestion." Jane Dormer nodded.

"Lady Jane, it is not a suggestion. It's a command, a royal command." She wheeled about quickly and faced Rose. "It's of particular importance that you give this message to Princess Elizabeth yourself. Others can take it to lower-ranking ladies of the court. Assure her that she can wear all the ruffs she wants—a dozen of them!" She gave a little squeal of laughter. "But no petal collars and no plum satin!" She tapped the fabric on the table with her finger. "You understand, Rose?"

"Yes, Your Majesty."

"She is under arrest right now at Hatfield, but she shall soon be transferred to Woodstock—a rather dreary, damp hunting lodge."

I get to go to Hatfield! Hatfield! To see Franny. And close to Dad!! But in the next moment her delight dissolved. She suddenly remembered that she had lied to her father and promised him she would never come back.

Chapter 25

The Hush Book

Hatfield House seemed to Rose like a ghost of its former self. There was only one lady-in-waiting in the presence room. She sat with her embroidery hoop next to Kat Champernowne, Elizabeth's former tutor. Though now bent with age, she looked up as Rose passed by.

"Oh, Rose! So nice to see you again. I heard you were coming with the fabric swatches."

"Yes, ma'am."

"My goodness, I haven't seen you in a while. You don't look a day older than the first time you came to Hatfield. I think the princess will be happy to see you." She paused. "And obedient to whatever commands the queen has for appropriate attire for the wedding."

"Yes," Rose replied softly. "Might I ask you, ma'am, does Franny Corey still work here?"

"Franny . . . Franny," Kat Champernowne said dimly. "Oh, you mean the scullery girl. The one who limps."

"Yes."

"I'm sure she does. She's probably doing five other jobs in addition to the scullery, as we are on a greatly reduced staff here." She sighed. "Not good times." The other lady who was stitching on her needlepoint hoop looked up. *A spy!* thought Rose. Jane the Bald had warned her when she had left Beaulieu that there were more spies at Hatfield than servants. Spies and numerous guards, as Princess Elizabeth was, after all, under arrest.

"But I think the princess is waiting for you. She is so excited about her dear sister's wedding." Kat cast her eyes toward the supposed lady-in-waiting. "So you'd best run along." She tipped her head toward the door of Elizabeth's apartments. "You might find the princess a bit changed."

"Changed" was an understatement, thought Rose as she faced the princess. By her own calculations, Princess Elizabeth was twenty-two years old. But she looked much older now. Dangerously thin, with a terrible yellowish pallor. Little lines, the ones people call crow's-feet, had begun to radiate out from the corners of her eyes. The princess looked straight at Rose, her mouth set in a grim line.

"As you can see, imprisonment in the Tower did me no favors. The apartments they assigned me were adequate enough, but it is unhealthy to live so close to the river. There is a miasmic fug that invades one's lungs." *Miasmic fug?* She had no idea what the princess was talking about. Must tell Mr. Ross for next week's word list. "The air is so bad it produces a catarrh. . . ." She began to cough. It took several seconds before she stopped. "The catarrh produces an excess of mucus in my throat, as you can tell from my voice. Kat tells me I should be bled."

"Oh, I don't think so!" Rose said with alarm.

Elizabeth looked at Rose with a mixture of curiosity and suspicion. "And why do you say that? You have a medical background?"

"No . . . no, but my mum . . ." Rose was winging it here. "My mum," she began again, "had a catarrh just like yours."

"Just like mine?" the princess said somewhat cynically. As if no one might dare have a disease that a royal had. *Oh, gimme a break!* Rose thought. Although she did feel sorry for the princess.

"Yes. And they decided to bleed her and she died, just like that," Rose said, snapping her fingers. There was no way that she would witness another bleeding. Dang! Some way, somehow, she was going to drag these people into twenty-first-century medicine. What if she got sick and they decided to bleed her! That was NOT going to happen.

"Well, shall we get on with it?" the princess said briskly. "Show me what I can and cannot wear to this . . . wedding. I understand that the handsome prince finally wrote her and also flung a few emeralds, rubies, and diamonds her way." Rose nodded, but she was surprised. The letter and gift had only happened the day before she had left Beaulieu to come to Hatfield. Elizabeth must have her spies too. Could it have been Jane the Bald? Bettina? Rose had suspected both of them for quite a while.

There was a tap on the door.

"Enter!"

It was Mrs. Dobkins! The head housekeeper was with another woman of about her age.

"Your Highness," Mrs. Dobkins said, and curtsied. So did the other woman. Then Mrs. Dobkins turned to Rose. "Rose, child, it's so good to see you again. You look the same as ever."

"I was about to comment myself on that," Elizabeth said. "She never seems to change, does she?" Rose felt panic streak through her.

"Good genes, I guess," she whispered.

"Good what?" Elizabeth asked.

"Oh . . . oh, my mother's name was Jeanne. I was just blessing her for her robust health."

"I thought she died of a catarrh when they bled her?" Elizabeth asked.

"Er . . . well . . . uh." Rose had to think fast. "That was precisely the problem. They bled her. I honestly don't think she would have died. She'd never been sick a day in her life."

"Never mind that," Elizabeth said dismissively. "And this is the seamstress who was recommended?"

"Yes, ma'am." The plump lady standing beside Mrs. Dobkins curtsied. She had a distracting wart with a hair growing out of it above one eye.

"And you have experience with Italian fabrics? I ask because I have some left over from those my father once gave to me. Although I believe that Rose, along with those forbidden fabrics, has also brought some swatches of fabrics that my dear sister, the queen, has suggested might prove suitable for the wedding." The way Princess Elizabeth said "dear sister," it was as if two poison darts had been shot through the air.

"Yes, I have had some experience, ma'am."

"Some is quite enough, believe me. I think none of us has to go out of our way for this . . . this wedding."

Rose stepped forward. "I can show you the sketches I made for the queen's dress and the fabrics to be used, if you like."

"Certainly." Princess Elizabeth gestured toward a long table.

Rose unfurled the parchment with the design she had

sketched in charcoal. And then she laid out the fabrics that must be avoided per the queen.

"This plum color is for the skirt and bodice. It's satin with an overlay of a soft gold in a tangled rose and leaf design. And the inset in the front of the skirt is bright gold cloth, which I believe will set off the plum color. The sleeves are cone with insets as well, in gray taffeta." Rose continued to explain the other details of the dress and then presented a list of forbidden fabrics and design elements signed by Sir Edward, the master of the queen's wardrobe.

Elizabeth read them. Silently her mouth curled into a sneer. "Petal collar. My my," she said softly. "Won't that chicken neck of hers look lovely in that." She rolled the list up and thwacked it against the palm of her hand.

"All right!" she said with a small note of triumph in her voice, then looked at Rose. "Rose, you have a keen eye for fashion and you are familiar with my style, my look. Might you have any suggestions?"

"Well, Your Highness, as I have said in the past, the queen seems to like very ornate styles. You see how her dress will be embellished with huge clusters of pearls. But do you remember the draping wing-style sleeve that I made for you those years back at Hatfield?"

"Oh yes, you called them the Princess Leia–style sleeve, based on some obscure fairy tale your mother told you."

"Indeed, ma'am. I would suggest something like that.

Therefore you avoid entirely the cone sleeve, which as you can see from the list is forbidden. As a matter of fact, I would think you should avoid any rich colors. Perhaps just white."

"White?"

"It's simple and pure. As a matter of fact"—Rose tapped her chin as if in deep thought—"I think white could become very popular in the future for weddings—especially for brides."

"Really?" Elizabeth said.

"Yes, very—how should I put it—fashion forward."

"Fashion forward—what a peculiar phrase, but quite descriptive, I think. I can just imagine a bride in a white gown on a white horse charging forward!" the princess exclaimed gaily, and laughed.

"Bless you, child," Mrs. Dobkins whispered as Rose left the room. "That is the first time I've heard the royal princess laugh in months."

Princess Elizabeth fell asleep dreaming of a white gown that would make her half sister look like the tawdriest bride in Christendom in that plum-colored atrocity of a wedding dress. Outside the palace the summer night hung with flickering fireflies as Franny Corey walked home toward the tiny thatched cottage where she lived with her parents. In a hidden pocket she had sewn into the coarse wool of her skirt was a Bible, and she felt the pleasant weight of it thumping against her thigh. Hush books, they were called. Small, easily tucked away in the crannies of a cottage or beneath the floorboards, these books were clung to by the secret worshippers, the remnant Protestants who were stubbornly resisting the queen's return to Catholicism and the pope.

As she walked, Franny knew that her parents suspected that she attended the secret prayer meetings and would be furious. Furious not because they were devout Catholics; anything but. However, they were fearful of the danger. The Coreys, after all, were time migrants themselves. They had fled a future century, one hundred forty years ahead of this one in England. Franny's home century was not the twenty-first, like her best friend Rose Ashley's, but the seventeenth. The year they had left was 1692. They had escaped from Salem, Massachusetts, on the eve of what would have been her mother's hanging for witchcraft. Her mother was of course not a witch at all, but a serious God-fearing woman of the Protestant faith. Her grandparents had gone to the New World of America more than a half century before, with a band of Puritan pilgrims on the *Mayflower*. They had gone for religious freedom. But now the family was back where the flight of their ancestors had begun, being persecuted again.

Sometimes Franny was unsure if she felt twelve years

old or one hundred fifty. Traveling through time, though quick, was in some ways endless. Was she just going around in circles? If she dared go back, would it be to that dreadful autumn night when her mother would be taken with four other witches to Gallows Hill? Twelve people had been hanged by that time. And one pressed to death with stones. Her uncle Giles Corey.

"Safe, Franny, we're safe," her mother kept muttering every time she brought up the subject. "Only God can see into your heart. He knows what your true faith is. You don't need to seek out these meetings."

"But Mum," Franny argued, "they're just meetings, not services."

"It doesn't matter, Franny," her father interrupted. "If you fall under suspicion, they won't care what you're doing if they discover you with like-minded Protestants."

But Franny did go to the meetings, at least when they were somewhat close to Hatfield. Now she was on her way back from a lambing shed where Master John Cabot, a yeoman farmer, had held a meeting. Not really a service, she had persuaded herself. They never said the Our Father out loud, at least. Though many mumbled it very quietly to themselves. Not Franny!

Rose Ashley knew Franny's story as Franny knew Rose's. Franny had told Rose everything about her life in Salem during that dreadful year. Franny was shocked when

Rose told her that in fact she had been to Salem with her own mother. They had taken a tour and actually gone to Gallows Hill, where so many had been hanged.

"A terrible place," Franny had muttered.

"You won't believe what's there now," Rose had said.

"What?"

"A Walgreens."

"What's a Walgreens."

Oh dear, Rose thought. *How to explain?* "It's this store where you can go and buy medicine and a lot of different things like toothbrushes and toothpaste, and toilet paper and candy. . . ."

Franny shook her head in dismay. "I have no idea what you are talking about, but it sounds better than gallows and people hanging in the air."

"Believe me, it is."

It was funny how that conversation drifted back to Franny. It must have been several years ago when Rose first came.

"Franny!" A voice threaded out of the blue summer night. She gasped.

"Rose—Rose Ashley!" How odd. She had been just thinking about Rose and now here she was. Could it be true?

"Oh, Franny!"

Franny tried to hasten her own pace, but with her lame

leg she simply could not run. Nevertheless she lurched ahead. Within five seconds Rose was embracing her. Together they tumbled to the ground, laughing.

"You're back!" Franny yelped. "It seemed like forever." Unlike the other people who knew Rose in this century and never seemed to notice her absences, Franny did. Rose felt it was because Franny herself was a time traveler. This tangled time seemed to have rules or principles of its own.

"Yes, yes, I'm here but just briefly."

"Why did you come?"

"The queen."

"She's here?" Franny's voice grew taut.

"Oh no. It's just that, well, you know she's to be married next month and I was charged with bringing the sketches and fabric samples of the wedding dress here to show Princess Elizabeth and . . ."

"She doesn't want Elizabeth to outshine her."

"Exactly. No one must wear the same color or have the same cut to their gowns."

"Does your father know you're here?"

"No, Franny, and you must not tell him." She paused as she saw the book on the ground beside Franny, where she had tumbled. "What's this?" she said, picking it up. Franny snatched it from her. But Rose knew in an instant what it was.

"Franny, you can't. You simply cannot own a Bible."

"But I do, Rose." She looked at her steadily. "I do." In a gentler voice she reached out and touched Rose's hand. "And you taught me how to read!"

"But that was before, long before Mary became queen."

"I'm not going to stop, Rose."

"It's simply too dangerous, Franny. If you were caught, it would be terrible. It's a crime to worship the way you do. To own this book." She tapped it with her finger. "My father was so frightened, he told me that I had to go back home, to my own time. That the queen was gathering kindling, kindling to burn Protestants. And you remember Sara, don't you?"

"Yes, she served alongside you in the princess's wardrobe, then went with you to serve the queen."

"Yes. And I think she suspects me of not following the faith. I am fearful she could report me."

"Sara? You never know about people, do you?"

"No, you don't."

"I always thought maybe Sara might be jealous of you. You had risen so quickly in Princess Elizabeth's favor as a wardrobe maid, then seamstress." Franny paused. "So why did you come back?"

"To see you. I was worried."

"To see me but not your father?"

"Well, I want to see him. But I sort of lied to him."

"Sort of?" Franny asked.

Rose giggled softly when she remembered what her father had said before. *You are no better a liar than your mum was.* "I kind of promised to stay away. But I really want him to come back with me. I want to try to persuade him and you. . . . You could come back with me too."

Franny shook her head. "I don't think so, Rose. If I tried to go back with you, I could very possibly end up in my home century. Once you become a migrant, it's very bad to go to another time other than your own century. Your father might be luckier. He has never gone to your century. But if he did, and for some reason he wanted to leave, he would end up right back here again. With luck, maybe Mary would no longer be queen."

Rose sighed. She felt the threat of tears building, welling up in her eyes. "But I wouldn't want him to go back here. I'd want him to stay and be my dad, in my century. I wouldn't want you to go back to Salem, but to come with me, come live in the future."

"It's impossible, Rose." She took Rose's hand again. "Rose, you must go back. I'll miss you dearly, but you have to go back before it gets too dangerous."

"But what about you, Franny? You've come from one of those meetings, haven't you?"

Franny nodded but would not meet Rose's eyes with her own.

"Can't you just go to Mass and pretend? You know, cross

your fingers when they say those prayers? Just pretend. It's just a smidgen of their religion while you have your own, tucked safely inside of you."

"That's what my mum says. You sound just like her. She says only God can see into your heart. He knows what your true faith is."

"Your mom is right. Totally. You have to get rid of this book. It's a death sentence."

"I'll think about it. I'll hide it somewhere where no one will find it."

"Not good enough, Franny,"

"It has to be good enough for now, Rose."

Chapter 26

The
Wedding

It was the first time Sara had seen Rose since she'd been back. They had adopted a manner of living close to one another but rarely speaking. Now they sat across from each other at a long worktable. Another seamstress, a woman large with child, stood up and stretched her back. Her name was Rowan. "I really can't believe it. But that is the last pearl I just stitched on the gown. We've actually completed this gown in time, good ladies! And now I can go have my baby in peace."

"And just think, here we are in Winchester. If you have the baby while we're still here for the wedding, the archbishop can baptize it!"

"Honestly, Sara, that is the least of my concerns. I'd

much rather be in my home village with my husband than here next door to the cathedral. I don't need a fancy bishop to baptize my babe."

Sara looked up from her needle and thread. "Mind your tongue, Rowan. You skirt blasphemy."

Rowan's mouth dropped open. "Imagine that—a woman ten years younger than me, ne'er married, ne'er given birth to anything beyond this dress, telling me how to bear a child and where!" Rowan stabbed her needle into a pincushion. An awkward silence welled up in the stuffy workroom.

Rose coughed a bit. "What I can't believe," Rose replied as she broke off a length of thread with her teeth, "is that the groom, Prince Felipe, has not yet shown up. Two days to go until the wedding, and they have not even met. Unbelievable."

The sewing room was in Wolvesey Castle, which had once been the palace of the Bishop of Winchester and was now housing the queen and her court. A large attic room had been converted to a workroom for Rose and six other seamstresses, who had been hired to help with the dress. They had worked night and day to finish it on time. Rain had been hammering down for days, it seemed, and when it stopped it was hot and muggy. The attic smelled like a locker room. And did anyone wear deodorant here? Of course not! Their remedy for underarm odor was a sprig of rosemary or mint. Rose shook her head and thought, *Doesn't work, ladies.* Of course, she probably stank herself.

They heard running steps coming up the staircase. It was Bettina. She burst into the room, her face flushed with excitement.

"He's here! The prince is here!"

"But it's close to midnight," Sara said. "Is she meeting him now?"

"You think she's going to wait one minute, let alone until morning, after all this time?" another woman, Edith, said, barely disguising a sneer.

Sara shot Edith a harsh look. "How unkind, Edith."

"Truth is often unkind," Edith retorted.

Oh, give me a break, Sara. Rose had immediately sized up Sara's role. She was the little Goody Two-shoes. The Goody Two-shoes with a dark heart and evil designs.

"Oh, Bettina, go to the room and find out what is going on," Rose urged.

"You think they're going to let me in the room? A dwarf. The queen doesn't want me tumbling around turning somersaults and those stupid tricks. She wants privacy."

But she was not going to get privacy. Unknown to the matrimonial couple, their first meeting was being observed by none other than Jane the Bald. The woman had a knack for eavesdropping, and a sixth sense about where to find a perch for such surveillance. The first thing Jane did when arriving in a new royal residence was to scout for such spots. As so many of these palaces and castles were old and in poor repair, it was never difficult to find such a place. She was happy that she did know more than a smattering of Spanish after all her years in service to Queen Mary. Before that she'd served her mother, Catherine of Aragon from Spain. The prince did not speak much English. So the couple conversed in three languages, actually—Spanish for the most part, but also small bits of Latin and some French. Mary could hardly restrain herself when he entered the room, and she raced forth to seize his hand and kiss it. The prince looked less enthusiastic. Jane couldn't wait to tell Rose. She had grown quite fond of the girl. Rose was not just smart, but clever beyond her years. Yet there was a mystery about her. Even Jane, who prided herself on being very perceptive, could not solve the mystery of Rose Ashley.

When the couple parted ways, Jane waited a few minutes before leaving her perch. She knew that Rose and the other seamstresses were still working into the wee hours, but she would wait until she heard them start to come down and then catch Rose's attention.

She had to wait almost an hour before she caught the sound of their feet. She spied Rose turning down a corridor.

"Psst!" Jane hissed. Rose turned around.

"It's me," Jane said, stepping out into the small pool of light cast by Rose's candle.

"Jane! What are you doing here?" Then she giggled. "I knew it. You spied on them, didn't you?"

"Indeed, my lass."

"What was it like? What happened?"

So Jane began to tell her all she had witnessed. Then, with a triumphant look on her face, she said, "But I save the best for the last."

"And what's that?"

"While I was waiting for you to come down, the prince came walking along that corridor that leads into this one. I was right around the corner just as the prince was coming along with one of his attendants. I heard him say that the queen was '*más vieja*' than he thought."

"*Más vieja*? What's that?"

"Much older than he thought. And that '*el tiempo no ha favoricido mucho a ella.*'"

"Huh?"

"Time had not been kind to her."

"Well, that's the truth." Rose sighed. "Not exactly a marriage made in heaven, I guess."

"No. Sounds like hell to me." Jane cackled.

The eyes should have been on the bride. And they were, for the first minute. It took only a minute, perhaps two at the most, for the wedding guests to discover Princess Elizabeth dressed in a stunning yet simple white gown. In contrast to the queen's encrusted plum satin gown with the overlay of embroidery and slashed with gold insets, the royal princess was like a calm beacon of light. Then when Prince Felipe handed off his mantle of cloth of gold, and people saw he was wearing a white doublet and white breeches, there was a slight gasp. Edith leaned over and whispered in Rose's ear, "And to think you trooped all over the countryside showing the queen's dress design and the swatches of fabric!" The princess certainly followed orders. "What could be more different?"

Rose, with the other seamstresses, peered from the open door of the sacristy where the church's bishop prepared for services.

"Look, they go together, the prince and the princess— a matched pair like eggs and bacon. Needle and thread," said Thelma, known for her intricate stitchery. "Milk and cream!"

"How romantic." Rowan giggled.

Sara shot her a dark look.

He might be milk or cream, thought Rose. But not Elizabeth. He was no match for her. She had recovered her beauty and vitality since Rose had last seen her at Hatfield. This prince was weak. And Elizabeth was growing stronger by the minute. She was surveying the crowd gathered for her hated half sister's wedding. Rose knew what was to come in just a few years. But the princess did not. Yet she seemed to be crackling to get there. She would. She was the Virgin Princess now, but within four years, upon the death of the Burning Queen, Elizabeth would be the Virgin Queen.

But four years seemed forever to Rose, and so many awful things would happen. Of course, it could be just a minute in tangled time. She watched as the wedding ceremony came to a conclusion. The bride turned now to walk down the aisle with her new husband. She caught a glimpse of Elizabeth.

"Uh-oh," Rose whispered to herself. The queen's eyes blazed, and for a moment it was as if the tiara she wore ignited into a nimbus of flames. The rose locket that hung from her neck glowered at her throat. Rose was transfixed. A paralysis crept through her. *I have to get out! I have to!*

Rose blinked. She was standing in front of the graftling. It looked healthier—just a bit. Her cell phone was next to the tray. Darn. She had wanted to try taking it with her and sneaking some pictures. But she had forgotten it. It would have been so cool if she had had pictures of the dress and the wedding. She wasn't sure how she would have sneaked it out to take a picture with no one noticing, but there were plenty of times when she had been alone. Now, however, she wondered how she had been transported back so quickly. She supposed that was always the way it happened. When she was least expecting it, she was just back! Unlike when she wanted to go the other way, back to the sixteenth century, which she could plan somewhat. She could go to the greenhouse, and if she concentrated on the damask roses, she could get there. But returning was a different story. It seemed very random.

She went back upstairs. Marisol was still sound asleep. *Let's see*, Rose thought. It would be another six hours until the alarm clock rang and they'd be off to school. There would be the new word list test. And in science—yuck—they were going to be dissecting a cow's eye. Before lunch, too. What an appetite killer that would be.

Chapter 27

Living in
Two Worlds

"*And now, class,*" *Ms. Elfenbach, the math teacher, said,* "*I've* saved the best for the last. Guess what happens today."

"What?" Susan asked.

"Based on the qualifying tests for Indiana State Middle Grade Mathlete Team, I am proud to say that we have two new members of the team from our seventh-grade class. I'd like to announce their names."

There was a buzz of excitement in the room. Rose knew she would not be one. Math was not her strong point. Joe leaned over and whispered, "I think we can relax on this one, Rose," with a chuckle.

"So right!" Rose replied. She knew that there was no

way her name would be announced, but she hoped Anand would make it again, and Sayid too.

"So let's give a big welcome to Susan Gold, on the team for the first time."

"Hooray . . . go Susan!" the class broke out.

"And . . . our returning team members, Anand, Myles, and Sayid Nassim!" Rose glanced over at Carrie. The color was draining from her face. Carrie was a standout math student. She had been on the team the previous year. And her sister, who was older, had been on the high school team for three years running. "And finally, our last mathlete—and I have to say I am particularly proud to announce this name—Marisol Juanita Esteban." There was a roar from the entire class. But Carrie's name was not among those called. "Welcome to the team. Our first practice session will be today after school."

Rose reached across the aisle and grabbed Marisol's hand. "This is so great! Listen, don't worry about the after-school practice. Calvin can swing by and pick you up after picking me up from my riding lesson."

"Okay. I can't quite believe it!"

"Me neither!" A scathing whisper. It was Carrie, of course, who gave them both a withering look.

"What's the problem?" Joe asked.

"Not exactly an all-American team," Carrie said.

Susan blinked. "What are you saying, Carrie?"

"Oh, you're okay, Susan."

"No, I'm not okay. What is your issue now, Carrie?"

"Forget about it."

Susan stood up. "No, Carrie. Take back what you just said."

"I never take anything back!" God, thought Rose, Carrie looked just like Sara in that moment. The same predatory light suffused her eyes.

Carrie turned her back and walked out of the classroom.

"There goes trouble," Susan said. "Come on. Let's go to lunch."

When they left the classroom, they saw that Brianna had pulled Carrie over and was speaking intensely to her. Lisa stood beside her. Carrie gave Brianna a light shove. "Just get out of my way."

"Yeah," said Tinker Bell, who had just come up to the two girls.

"Ugh!" Rose exhaled loudly. Jenny turned around and looked at Rose.

"Jenny," Rose said, "you should avoid those girls. They're toxic."

"Stay out of this, Rose. Go back to your stupid fashion blog," Carrie said, then wheeled about and saw Sayid staring at her. "And what are you staring at, Sayid? Why don't you just go home? As in, where you came from. Syria, Egypt, wherever—in the desert. I'm sure they're short of mathletes in the desert!" A cold dread flooded through Rose.

Marisol pulled Rose away. "Let's go to lunch."

No one talked much at lunch. It should have been celebratory, but Carrie's toxicity had seeped into the air at their usual lunch table with Anand, Sayid, Joe, Myles, Kevin, Marisol, and Susan.

"She is such a colossal jerk," Joe said.

A jerk is one thing, thought Rose. *She's dangerous*. She had to take Susan aside and talk to her about how Marisol's papers were coming along. She had a very bad feeling. Time was of the essence.

"I wanted to tell to her that my parents are citizens," Sayid said. "And I am too. My father pays taxes to the United States government."

"She wouldn't listen," Susan said.

Marisol shook her head. "I don't want to talk about this."

Once Rose was in the car with Calvin on her way to Hunter Valley Riding Academy, she took out her cell phone and called Susan.

"So, Susan, what should we do if the immigration people come to our door?"

"Don't let them in. You don't have to. Tell Betty, tell

your grandmother, tell everyone who works for your grandmother."

"Wait a second. I'm going to put you on speakerphone
so Calvin can hear this."

Calvin leaned closer to Rose. "Hi, Susan. I'm listening.
All ears here."

"You don't have to open the door unless they show a
warrant. And you can ask them to slide that under the door.
And then, this is the most important thing of all . . . if
they come in, you can remain silent. That is your right.
You don't have to sign anything or speak until you have a
lawyer there with you. I'm going to text you my dad's office
number and cell in case any agents show up. My dad is at
your grandmother's, explaining all this to her."

"What's taking so long with all the papers and forms?
Why can't all this just happen?"

"I don't know. But Dad will get Marisol through all
this. Just don't panic."

"I'm not panicking, but I am really worried about Carrie. You know how she is."

"Look, what's the worst she can do?"

"I don't even want to imagine, Susan." She looked out
the window. They were turning through the gates of the
riding academy. "Got to go."

Rose turned to Calvin. "You got all that about Marisol?"

"Don't worry, Rose. We've got Marisol covered."

"Yeah, but I do worry. You know how Gran has those spells. Just the other day she forgot who Marisol was."

"Well, that might be good. If these agents come to the house and ask for Marisol Esteban and your grandmother says, 'Never heard of her,' they might think they have the wrong house altogether."

"Hmmm . . ." Rose thought. Calvin had a point. It would be like, *Marisol who?* As if she didn't exactly exist. The idea of tucking Marisol away in a distant century—at least until the papers could be squared away—was becoming increasingly appealing. Could she persuade Marisol? That was the problem. Marisol wanted to be where her mom was, in a country that was safe, where there was no war. But not a different century. There was not exactly war now in Bolivia, but there were drug gangs and violence and poverty.

Rose was thinking of all this as she walked into the changing room at the riding academy. Just as she opened the door, she heard giggling. She waited a moment and listened.

"Jamie works in the stables. He's just kind of an assistant to Peter, the riding teacher, but he's so cute, Jenny. I think maybe he likes me just a little bit."

"How old is he?"

"Fifteen."

"That's so much older than you."

"Not that much. He just turned fifteen and I'll be thirteen next week. Oh yes, by the way, I'm inviting you to my birthday party next week. You're the only sixth grader I'm inviting. Carrie says it's okay."

"Really! Lisa. Oh, you're so . . . so . . ."

"Evil," Rose said, barging into the changing room. Jenny froze. Then her eyes began to dart back and forth between Rose and Lisa. The glitter sparkled in her topknot. "Oh, and speaking of evil—that glitter's been declared an environmental hazard. Its microplastic fragments can be inhaled. So, as the saying goes, 'all that glitters is not gold.' It's toxic. You wouldn't want to hurt a horse, would you?"

"Come on!" Lisa grabbed Jenny by her shoulder, and they ran out of the changing room.

"Oh, Jamie," Rose heard Lisa cooing. "This is my friend Jenny."

"Hi, Jenny."

"She's going to take her first riding lesson today with Christina."

"Oh yeah. Christina's great. But maybe you better put a helmet on or comb some of that glitter out of your hair. Christina doesn't like that stuff around the horses."

Yay! Rose pumped her fist into the air and gave a small leap. *Vindicated!* she thought. It was a word from this week's word list.

She came out of the changing room just as Lisa and Jenny were coming back in.

"Hi, Rose," Jamie said. "It's great to see you again. Seems like forever."

"Yeah, well, there's been a lot of snow. We couldn't get out here."

"I know—I couldn't either. This place basically shut down for almost two weeks."

Whenever Rose saw Jamie, she thought of Andrew. Andrew had worked in the saddlery and the stables of Hatfield. They looked quite a bit alike. Andrew had been perhaps seventeen when Rose first met him. He had taken her for being older, because of her height. But when she had glimpsed him the last time she'd gone to Hatfield, she had been shocked. Like the princess, he had aged. He now looked close to thirty. Still very handsome. He too would have most likely said, "Oh, Rose, you haven't changed a bit." It was always awkward, as she never knew what to say back. The truth was that everyone had changed except her. She wondered what it would have been like for her mom to go back and see her father aging while she stayed the same. She had noticed the last time she and her father had met that he had a few more gray hairs in his sideburns. But she pushed the thought out of her mind.

Rose saddled Ivy, mounted up, and proceeded to one of the indoor rings, where Peter, her riding teacher, was waiting. She went through the usual exercises before the jumping part of the lesson began. She heard the clunk of Ivy's hind hooves on the bar.

"You're too far forward in the saddle, Rose. You're hanging on Ivy's neck. Not good."

Rose sighed. She didn't get much better. Her mind was definitely elsewhere. At the end of the lesson she came to the center.

"A little distracted, and a bit rusty," Peter said to her. "But you'll get it back. Not to worry."

It seemed to Rose that everyone was telling her not to worry today. But she was worried—too many people she loved were in danger. Living in two worlds was harder than she would ever have imagined.

Chapter 28

The
ICE Men

"I *feel . . . I feel . . ."* *Rosalinda was bent over a tray of seedlings with* a magnifying glass. "The beginnings of spring." She paused. ". . . Or is it a false spring?" Outside there was the soft patter of a drizzly rain

"What are you talking about, Gran?" Rose looked up from the seedlings that she was tying to slender sticks.

"Mud-lucious coming."

Oh dear, thought Rose. *She's going off again.* Tangling words, forgetting names. She had to get her back on track.

"Gran, mud what? What kind of name is that? Who are the mud-lucious?"

Rosalinda threw up her hands. "Oh, my dear girl. You think that's a name. It's just a word. So perfect for these almost-spring days. You never heard that poem about just spring?"

"No, Gran. But it's just February now."

"Well, there is a poem that is the best poem ever written about spring. It's by a very famous poet, E. E. Cummings, who died, I don't know, maybe seventy years ago."

How could her grandmother remember the name of a poet who died that long ago and not Marisol's name, who lived right in her own house?

"Do you remember the poem?"

Her gran shrugged. "A bit."

"Can you say it to me, maybe?"

Rosalinda set down the magnifying glass and, closing her eyes, folded her hands primly in her lap. She took a deep breath.

"in Just-
spring when the world is mud-
luscious the little
lame balloonman . . ."

She stopped abruptly. "Oh, I forget." She sighed. "I'll tell you, Rose, getting old isn't for sissies."

"You're no sissy, Gran."

This might be a good time to test her grandmother. She had been drilling her as to what she should do if the

Immigration and Customs Enforcement men came to their door.

"Gran, can we go over what you're supposed to say if the Immigration and Customs guys come here?"

"Oooh, *The ICE Men Cometh.* One of my favorite plays." Her gran always said this whenever they mentioned Immigration and Customs. "Yes, of course. I have the right to remain silent about . . ." She looked up blankly. "What's her name again?"

"Marisol Esteban, but don't say her name to them. You just say, 'I have the right to remain silent until my lawyer is present.'"

"Good, I'll say that. I have the right to remain silent until my lawyer . . ." Her eyes darted around a bit as if searching for Sam Gold's name. "Until Thomas Cromwell is present."

Rose gasped. "No, Gran, Thomas Cromwell was you-know-who's minister."

"Oh, of course, Henry, King Henry the Eighth. Ours is Gold, right?"

"Right, Gran. Just remember you can just shut your mouth. It's not a crime."

"Not an off-with-your-head kind of crime."

"No, Gran."

"And the little girl upstairs—your friend—Marisol Esteban."

Betty had now shown up to take Rosalinda upstairs.

"Ready for bed, Mrs. A?"

"Not quite. Might you take me into the library? I need to look something up about the old bald men."

"What?" Rose and Betty said at the same time.

Rosalinda broke into gales of laughter. "Those pests in the potato seedling trays. That's what we called them way back when. I believe for some unknown reason they were called Jerusalem crickets. Today we just call them potato bugs. Ugly critters. About two inches long, beady black eyes. They attack potatoes and all sorts of tubers. They even attack their own. The females kill the males after mating. Chomp off their heads. Charming, isn't it?" She looked pointedly at Rose. "Like some monarchs we have heard of."

"Uh, okay, Gran. I'll see you in the morning."

Eventually Rose heard Betty walking toward the library door to look in on Rosalinda and see if she was ready to go upstairs. Rose continued checking the humidity in the seedling trays. She looked out to the back of the greenhouse. A thick fog swirled outside. The single streetlight appeared to float dimly in the shroud of fog like a gigantic pearl. A meow cut the soft patter of the drizzle on the glass panes of the greenhouse.

"September!" She was never sure if September came back with her. It seemed that sometimes she did and sometimes not. She walked over to the windows that looked out on the alley. In the faint illumination from the streetlight she saw a figure. The figure was holding September. But over her shoulder was a pair of ice skates. *Brianna! What is she doing here?*

Rose didn't even bother to get a coat. She went out the back door of the greenhouse.

"Why are you here on a night like this?"

"I . . . I have to tell you something . . . something bad."

Rose looked at her suspiciously and held out her arms for September, who leaped into them.

"What?" Rose said warily. Barely three months ago, on Halloween night, Brianna and the Mean Queens had chased her home after trick-or-treating. Chased her down this very alley and thrown a rock at her. It had barely missed her head, but had crashed into one of the greenhouse windows. September had leaped out at the girls and managed to claw Lisa's face, leaving an angry-looking scratch.

"Uh . . . ," Brianna began. "Are we going to stand out here in the rain?" September purred and looked up at Rose. *You want me to ask her in, don't you?*

"All right. Come into the greenhouse."

They entered. Brianna looked around. "This is really beautiful. I feel like I'm in another . . . country, almost."

"So what did you want to tell me that's so bad?"

She took a deep breath. "Carrie, Lisa, and that sixth

grader Jenny. Well, I kind of knew they were up to something. You know how Carrie gets."

"I do. Too bad it took you so long to figure it out."

"Yeah, well . . ." Brianna took a deep breath. "You know how crazy she is about not being on the mathlete team, going on about how it's not American enough or something."

"Yeah, or something," Rose said in disgust, rolling her eyes.

"So I pretended to be friends with them again."

"Are you sure you were pretending?"

"Yes," Brianna said fiercely. "I faked it. They had this big plan to rat out Marisol to the immigration people. They wanted me to dial the number and tell them everything. Your address, about your grandmother."

"You didn't!"

"I lied. I told them the number was out of order. The first time."

"The first time?"

"The next time I just dialed some random number and pretended to report it."

"And what happened?"

"Somehow they figured out that I had dialed some place that wasn't the real place. Not the immigration office.

"So today after school, Carrie sneaked into the school office and dialed the real number and reported that there was an illegal alien girl living at your address. Carrie didn't want it traced to her iPhone, which is why she used the school's phone."

"What? How did you find this out?"

"Jenny. Jenny is stupid and bribable."

"What did you bribe her with?"

"A promise that I could get her into the audition for *America's Next Top Tween Model*."

"Oh God, like Mia Ryles! The YouTube creep." Rose paused a second. "But can you?"

"Of course not."

"So what does all this mean?"

"It means that those agents from immigration could show up here any minute."

"OMG, I have to get Marisol!" It was as if Rose's heart had leaped to her throat. She looked around wildly, then tore out of the greenhouse and up the stairs to her bedroom.

She arrived, panting. "Marisol!"

"Yes?"

"Marisol, things are very dangerous. You have to come with me."

"Why?"

"They know you're here. The ICE men."

"No!"

"Marisol, I can keep you safe."

"Where?"

"It's too hard to explain right now. But it's safe. It's the safest place you'll ever be. Cross my heart and hope to die." She grabbed Marisol's hand and yanked her.

At the very moment they were at the top of the stairs, the doorbell rang.

"Now, who could that be at this time of night?" Betty said.

Rose froze. She and Marisol were at the top of the staircase, about to come down. They could hear the sound of Rosalinda's and Betty's footsteps as Betty helped her to the stair lift. The door opened.

A man's deep voice was heard. "Sorry to disturb you ladies. I'm Agent Sawacker from Immigration and Customs Enforcement. We understand that you have an illegal immigrant by the name of Marisol Juanita Esteban."

"What?" her gran's voice cawed.

"Marisol Juanita Esteban," the agent repeated.

"I know no one of that name. Not here, not anywhere."

"Are you sure?"

"Yes, I'm sure. And I'm also sure that I have to urinate very badly and don't want to wet this pair of diapers that my caretaker just changed an hour ago." Rose and Marisol looked at each other and almost laughed out loud.

"Oh!" the ICE man said.

"Oh! You say! Well, just you wait, young man, until

you're eighty-eight years old and your bladder is as leaky as an old tin can. Yes indeed, an eighty-eight-year-old bladder is not all fun and games!"

"Sorry to intrude, ma'am."

"I am too!" Rosalinda huffed.

Marisol breathed a sigh of relief.

"It's not over yet. Follow me," Rose said, still holding Marisol's hand tight in her own. "We're going down the back stairs to the greenhouse."

Three minutes later they were standing in front of the damask rose graftling. Rose shut her eyes momentarily and inhaled deeply.

"Okay, Marisol, what I'm about to tell you is going to sound really, really strange." Marisol nodded. "But there is something very special we share."

"Our friendship, Rose."

"Well, yeah, but something else too." She paused a second. "You see, Marisol, we are both migrants."

"I don't understand."

"Marisol, you are a migrant in place. But I am a migrant in time."

"What, Rose? You were born here in this country. What does that mean—migrant in time?"

"I was born here, as you say. But my father lives in another time."

Marisol's brow furrowed. "What do you mean, another time?"

"You know my mother died last summer in a car crash. She was born here too. If she had lived, she would have been forty-nine. But my father—that's a different story."

"What story is that, Rosa?"

"My father was born in the year 1504."

Marisol shook her head. "That's impossible! He would be over five hundred years old."

"But he's not. See, that's the strange thing. He's there. He's about fifty. He's fine. More than fine. He's the goldsmith for the royal court."

"Royal court?"

"Yes, the English court. Mary, the daughter of Henry the Eighth in England, is now the queen."

"And you've met this five-hundred-year-old father?"

"He's not five hundred. He's fifty, and yes, I've met him."

"How?"

"I told you. I'm a time migrant. So were my mother and my grandmother."

"Rosalinda?" Marisol began muttering softly to herself in Spanish. Then she looked up. "So you go to this place?" Rose nodded. "How?"

"The greenhouse here is a portal."

"Like a border?"

"Sort of, but not exactly. But I can get you there. I can hide you away. No one will ever find you. No one."

"Then not even my mother could find me, and I won't find her there either."

"But you'll be safe."

Marisol looked away from Rose. "No! No, Rose. I won't go."

"Please, Marisol."

"No, I told you, I'm staying here." And she stomped her foot.

Rose looked at her. She knew that there was no way she could persuade Marisol to go.

Rose sighed. "Okay. You go up to bed."

Marisol turned and began walking away, then turned and smiled at Rose. "*Dios bendiga la vejiga débil de tu abuela.*"

"What does that mean?"

"God bless your grandmother's weak bladder."

Rose rushed up to Marisol and embraced her.

The night, thought Brianna, *is a lonely place when the stars don't shine.* No one was at Lake Marian tonight skating. There were no bonfires, no sledding. But the ice was still firm. She laced up her skates and glided out onto the lake. She had to think. When Brianna had told Rose the agents were coming, Brianna knew that for herself it meant much more. It meant that for the first time in her life she had done something good—not for herself but for someone else. She had taken a risk. A new kind of risk. Not a double axel skating trick. Not a be-the-most-popular-girl kind of risk, but something entirely different. She felt better than she had in a long time. But she didn't feel especially happy. She still felt a profound shame for what she had done and been in the past. She took the full blame for Joe's broken ankle. She didn't care about medals anymore, or competing someday in the state championships, the Nationals, or the Olympics. That didn't matter anymore. But still she was so achingly lonely. She felt engulfed in an ocean of loneliness. It washed through her like a rising tide—a tide in which she might drown. But she wasn't fearful. She felt at peace. And kept whispering to herself, 'I helped someone. I helped them.' She tipped her head up toward the drizzling night. No stars. Nothing.

There was a sharp *crack* from the ice. Her heart seemed to lurch. It was as if the earth had shifted beneath her skate blades.

Was this the end? Her end?

Whatever! she thought. She felt the water beginning to seep into her skates.

Chapter 29

The Scent of Smoke

"They say we'll be moving to Hampton Court for the confinement," Jane the Bald said as they rushed along a corridor in Whitehall Palace.

"Confinement? What is that?" Rose asked. A minute before, she had been standing in her grandmother's greenhouse, begging Marisol to come with her, and now she was here. In that strange way she had of vaguely knowing everything that had happened in her absence, she was quickly catching up. The events were coming into clearer focus.

"Confinement? You don't know the term?" Jane asked.

"Sort of." Rose fudged it a bit.

"Well, I suppose in the servant classes pregnant women

cannot afford to stay away and not work. But in court, and certainly with princesses and queens, they cannot be seen pregnant as the date of their child's birth approaches. It is considered immodest. You know, the big belly and all."

"Queen Mary has no belly as far as I can see. I have not been asked to let out any of her gowns since that ceremony thingamajig."

Jane unleashed a peal of laughter. "You have such a way with words, Rose. I assume you are referring to the quickening ceremony, to celebrate when the baby first kicked inside her belly."

"Yes, that's it." Rose had never seen such ridiculous goings-on in her life. There were jousting tournaments, a ball, and endless religious services—all in celebration of an unborn baby's first little kick or punch inside the womb.

"The quickening celebration was almost three months ago, Jane, and I haven't had to let out a dress of Her Majesty's since. She doesn't look any fatter to me."

"Nor to me either." Jane slowed her pace and drew Rose into a shadowy corner where the corridor turned into the long gallery that connected with the tennis courts. "Let me tell you," the queen's fool whispered. "You are not the only one with doubts. There are even rumors that a substitute baby will be swapped in at the time she is supposed to deliver."

"April, right near Easter, that's the time, isn't it?"

"Yes."

"I've been asked to make some cute baby smocks. You know, spring colors with a few Easter bunnies hopping around."

"Easter bunnies!" Jane's eyebrows shot up into that hairless desert of her head.

Uh-oh! Rose thought. She'd done it again. "It's . . . it's just a custom from my part of the country. West Ditch near Twickenham, you know." Rose blamed every modern phrase she accidentally uttered on West Ditch, her supposed home village.

Suddenly she got a whiff of a peculiar smell. Something was burning, but what? It sent a shiver through her. "What is that . . . that smell?"

Jane grasped her hand. "They did it!"

"Did what?"

Jane turned toward Rose. Her face was white as chalk. Her protuberant eye began to throb in a rhythm all its own. She raised her other hand toward her eye and covered it as if to calm it down. As if it had seen too much.

"Did what?" Rose asked in a strangled whisper.

"God rest ye, John Rogers."

"Who is he?"

"The first heretic to be burned. I didn't think they would actually do it."

"But where? How can we smell the fires from here?"

"Smithfield, where the pyres have been built for the heretics, is just two miles north of here. Must be a north wind blowing that brings this horrible smell."

"Pyres. They will burn more than one?"

"Indeed. I fear eight more are now awaiting their turn for the kindling to be lit."

"Oh, Jane!" Rose closed her eyes. Her father had warned her! But she had come back. And now was on her way to see the queen with a parcel of the latest smocks she had made for a baby. A baby whose mother had just given the order to set another human being on fire for not believing as she did. No God in any religion on earth would want this. Of this Rose was certain.

Rose and Jane walked on. Before they entered the presence room, they both looked at each other and took a deep breath. If the scent of smoke carried an excruciating message for Rose and Jane, the ladies-in-waiting of the presence room and the queen who sat in an elevated chair in the middle seemed completely immune. They were tending to their needlepoint and giggling as Bettina turned somersaults. Then she began a series of imitations of different animals as the women called out their choices.

"Do the frog, Bettina. We all love the frog." Rose felt a wave of nausea as she watched Bettina crouch down and begin to spring forward. These people were loathsome. They burned heretics and treated humans like toys. Bettina had achondrogenesis—yes, that was the name for dwarfism. Susan had an aunt who had this condition and had done a report on her for science class.

Rose turned to Jane and said, "I have to go—I'm going to be sick." She ran from the room.

Racing through the corridor, she managed to find a convenient urn into which to vomit. The smell was relatively sweet compared to the one outside. She then continued to her own quarters and sank down on the bed. "What have I gotten myself into?" She spoke to the air as if expecting an answer. On the small table that served as her desk lay a stack of rag paper. Sir Waldegrave had been very generous in giving her paper for her sketches of clothing designs. There was a sketch on top, a design for a christening gown for this stupid baby—a phantom baby, in Rose's mind.

She got up and went to the desk, tore up the paper, and looked at the blank one beneath it. She had forgotten yet again to bring her iPhone. Her departure had been too sudden, and she had had many thoughts swirling through her head. She sat down at the desk, picked up a quill, dipped it in an ink pot, and began to write. The scratchy sound of the goose quill was somehow soothing to her. She began with the first thought that came to her mind.

So they burned a man today. I can still smell the smoke. This makes me so worried—dared she write her name? Perhaps just the letter *F. When I got back here, I planned to bring Dad back home with me and to make sure that F is safe. I must know that before I leave. I doubt F would come back with me. She is like Marisol in this sense. Her father and mother are here in England, after all, and Marisol's mom is in America somewhere. F would no more come back with me to America than Marisol would go back to Bolivia. But Dad might be another story. I can only hope. I think I'm going to have to fess up and let Dad know I'm here. I can't stand telling a lie.*

Then there was a rap on the door.

"Yes, who is it?"

"Jane and Bettina."

"Come in!"

"How are you?" Jane looked anxious.

"Yes," Bettina said. "I saw you dash out of the presence chamber."

"I . . . I became ill. But I'm feeling better now." She discreetly folded the paper and tucked it under a blotter on the desk.

"The queen loved the little gowns and smocks for the baby, especially the ones with the bunny rabbits," Jane said. "As a matter of fact she immediately took to calling the child Bunny."

Oh God, I might throw up again, Rose thought.

"We go to Hampton Court soon. Three weeks or so, I believe," Bettina said. "More things are ordered for the royal birth."

"More clothes. This is going to be the most well-dressed baby ever. Thelma and I and the others are stitching away."

"Not just clothes ordered, but some jewelry too," Bettina said.

"Jewelry—a baby wears jewels?" But then Rose's mouth dropped open. She knew what Bettina was saying. It was code. This meant her father would be coming to Hampton Court!

"Yes," Bettina continued. "Many medals to be struck for the attending doctors and something as well for the midwives, and then of course the godparents. And we understand a rather large diamond ring for the father, Prince Felipe. He did what he was supposed to do. Produce an heir."

"We'll see." Jane sneered.

Rose thought her heart might leap out of her chest. Bettina was the only one who knew that Nicholas Oliver was her father. She did not know, though, that Rose was from another time and another place. That secret was one she had to keep. Bettina had proved herself to be a wonderful messenger between Rose and her dad, the royal goldsmith.

"So when do we go to Hampton Court?"

"The baby is due in April near Easter, and the queen's official confinement begins in a few days. So soon, I would imagine."

Soon, Rose thought. She would see her father and beg him to leave, to come back with her. She would apologize for defying his wishes. She cringed at the fact that she had lied to him, defied him. But it was for love. He had to understand. He just had to!

Chapter 30

Phantom Baby

The burnings have increased. Eight so far!! And even though we are at Hampton Court, as the queen's official "confinement" period has begun, if the wind blows the wrong way we can still smell that horrid odor of smoke and ash and burning flesh.

The queen seems not to smell it, and as far as I can tell she looks no bigger. If I were that baby, I wouldn't want to be born. Imagine having your first breath of air filled with the stink of these murders. Yuck! Of course some seem not to mind the stink—such as you-know-who—S, I shall call her. We don't speak anymore, but I saw her rushing down a long corridor the other day. She has become best friends with the queen's hairdresser. The odor was quite strong that day, and S stopped and inhaled deeply and said, "I know some people complain about the fires, but I find the fragrance fortifying. Purifying, almost, for our land is being rid of a terrible pestilence." And all the hairdresser said was "Well, I have a cold today and my nose is all stuffed up. Can't smell a thing. Not a roasting pig or a roasting human." Imagine that—the horror!

I think Dad is coming today to deliver the medallions—or so Bettina says. I have to figure out how and where to meet him. Will he be mad? I think I can explain it. And I do hope he'll have some news about Franny. Must finish this. Due in the queen's presence room at 11:00. The clock in the court is now chiming the quarter hour.

I do wonder about Marisol and Gran. I know I have only been gone a minute or two in their time, yet I have been here for more than a month. My! The entanglements of time.

"Entanglement"—that was a word on Mr. Ross's most recent word list. I wonder if I'd get a bonus point for using it in a different century?

Fifteen minutes later, Rose was entering the presence room to show Her Majesty the Queen two possible christening gowns. One if the child was a girl and one if a boy.

Rose was motioned to the front of the room, where Queen Mary reclined on a daybed with her hands calmly folded over her belly—her rather small belly.

She appeared to be dictating a letter to one of her secretaries, who sat at a small desk.

"'Your Holiness,

"'I hope this finds you in excellent health. I am sure you will rejoice in the joyous news of the safe delivery of our child. As of'—just put a blank line for the date, Sir Thomas—'a sweet infant was born at'—just fill in the date, and the hour. And the gender and name." She turned her head toward her husband, Prince Felipe. "I think it's a nice detail to put in the hour and even the minute, don't you think so too, Felipe?"

"Of course, my dear," the prince answered in a bored voice, and could barely conceal a yawn.

"So, Sir Thomas, just leave that blank, then go on." She sighed. "Then write, 'I'm sure you will rejoice and be pleased with God's infinite goodness in the happy delivery of our son/daughter. Most sincerely, Mary, Queen of England, France, Naples, Jerusalem, and Ireland, Princess of Spain and Sicily, Archduchess of Austria, Duchess of

Burgundy, Milan, and Brabant, Countess of Hapsburg, and lawful wife of the most noble and virtuous Prince Felipe by the same Grace of God.'" She paused to take a breath. "Now be sure copies of that are sent to the pope, also to the king of France, the Austrian emperor, and the rest of the lot." She waved her hand dismissively. At that moment a lady-in-waiting approached and whispered something to the queen. The queen clapped her hands in delight. "Do send her in."

Rose was signaled by Jane Dormer to step back to make way for the new visitor. The visitor came forth. Or rather waddled forth. It was a ruddy-faced woman the likes of whom had never been in a palace of any kind, let alone the presence room of a queen. She was carrying something in her arms. Jane Dormer now stepped up to the queen.

"Your Majesty, allow me to present Matilda Cooper with her three babies, delivered just two days ago."

"Mrs. Cooper, do come closer and let me see your precious darlings. I understand that you are of an age close to mine."

"Yes, ma'am, I mean, Your Majesty." She gave a small curtsy.

"And look at you, up and about and looking so fine."

"Well, you know, ma'am, after you've had eight children, three more don't make no difference really."

"Oh!" Mary's laughter tinkled pleasantly in the room. "Charming."

Charming, thought Rose. What is charming about having eight children when one is a peasant and must exist on the smallest amounts of food from whatever little plot they could cultivate? Franny's parents only ate meat perhaps twice a year.

Rose peeked around the woman's broad back as she uncovered the triplets for the queen to see. They were robust little creatures. One yawned, one gurgled, and one began howling bloody murder. Then, Jane Dormer signaled that the woman should take them away. Which she immediately did. A great look of relief swept across the mother's face. By the time she left the room, all three were howling.

Chapter 31

Fire
and Ice

April 13, 1555. So Easter has come and gone and no
little Easter bunny has shown up. We are now in the
third week of April. But you know who else hasn't
shown up? Dad. He was supposed to come last
week but it rained constantly and the roads were
impassable. Bettina tells me she's sure he'll come
this week. . . . Thank heaven Easter has passed. The
High Masses for Easter go on forever. Especially
the one that starts on Saturday, three hours before
midnight. My knees are killing me still. But guess
who was watching me the whole time. S! Of course.
The queen got a special dispensation from the

pope to sit this service out because of her delicate condition. She didn't exactly sit it out, though. An altar on wheels was brought into her apartments. Pays to have friends in high places—like the pope. And be assured I don't mean God. I don't think God is exactly Mary's friend. If he is, I am profoundly disappointed in him. There have been ten more burnings!

There are whispers that Prince Felipe has a crush on Princess Elizabeth, but rumor has it that the princess thinks he's kind of weird, and besides, she likes Robert Dudley, who is OMG so cute!! Isn't this sounding more and more like middle school texting? Except it's not texting. I'm writing this on a piece of ancient rag paper with a goose quill and a kind of ink made from something called iron vitriol and crunched-up oak galls, those big knobby things that grow on tree. Definitely a lot harder than texting!

April 20, 1555. Still no baby, but yes more burnings. I feel that I am living in two different realities here. Imagine a queen who orders people to die, yet at the same time is so excited about the coming birth of her child. But nobody really believes that the baby is coming. "A figment of her imagination," Jane says. Well, I want to say to the queen, "Imagine what it's like being tied to a stake, then have bundles of twigs and reeds laid at your feet." And I was told that often they tie bags of gunpowder between the victim's knees to ensure that the person was not only burned but blown to bits.

Rose would never have dared to keep such a diary if she had not been living alone in this room. Thankfully, Sara had been moved to another part of the palace. They had not spoken a single word since that night Sara had come into her room and accused her of having a Bible. They didn't have to work in the wardrobe on the queen's clothes either, as Sara had been sent to the nursery, where she was now being tutored on the care of an infant by an old nurse-maid of the late King Edward. Grammy Nonny, as she was called, was considered an expert in newborns and child-hood illnesses—of which Edward had had many.

Rose's nub of a candle was now burning low. But so disturbed were Rose's thoughts that she was uncertain she could sleep, and she wondered how long she had been here in England, in the court. She had arrived in early February, and it was now May. But this might only translate to three or four minutes away from her grandmother's house. She hoped that Marisol was still safe—for three minutes she should be. She wondered about the graftling. It seemed it might have grown a bit, become a little less droopy. Nevertheless, she felt a peculiar unease. She snuffed out the last flicker of the candle stub, got up from her desk, then put on her night hood and climbed into bed. She was not sure what was disturbing her, causing this disquiet.

Despite this unease Rose fell asleep almost instantly. Hours later something blue, bright blue, and pulsing, flashed through her dreams, and then a high shrill sound—a siren! She sat straight up in bed. This was crazy. There were no sirens here. Nor were there flashing blue lights. This was an ambulance. But the word was written backward, just as it was on an ambulance, so that drivers could read it in their rearview mirrors.

ƎƆИA⅃UBMA

Her heart seemed to skip a beat, or maybe two. This was not a dream. This was real. This was happening in her home century, at 4605 North Meridian Street, Indianapolis, Indiana 46204. She had to get back! Right now. But sometimes it was harder getting back than leaving. *Calm down. You can do this.* She shut her eyes tightly. She imagined the greenhouse. Nothing happened. Then the thought of the graftling came to her—fragile and trembling in an odd breeze. She felt something cool against her face. Had she left the window open on this warm June night? And then another sensation, the soft brush of September's tail!

She was back. Standing with the cat in her arms. The throbbing blue lights of an ambulance swept through the greenhouse. She put September down and ran to the entry hall of their house. Two men, emergency medical technicians, were lifting a stretcher. Rosalinda was on it. Marisol stood as if nailed to the floor with her hands lifted to her mouth, as if muffling a silent scream. Betty was beside the stretcher.

"What happened?" Rose asked.

"Not sure," Betty answered. "I think it might be just one of her spells."

"I want to go with her," Rose said, stepping close to the stretcher.

"Stand back, miss, please," one of the EMTs said.

"Who are you?" the other asked.

"I'm her granddaughter."

"Let her come?" Rosalinda said in a breathy voice.

All the way to the hospital, Rose held her gran's had. They had put an oxygen mask on her and already hooked her up to an intravenous tube.

"Gran, you're going to be okay. I just know it. I'm here. I won't leave your side. I promise." Gran's lips moved but no sound came out. "Don't try to talk, Gran. Just save your strength."

There was the scream of another siren coming.

"Busy night," one of the EMTs said.

"A call from the park ranger's office. Some fool fell through the ice on Lake Marian."

"Who'd be stupid enough to go out on a night like this on that ice? Everything's thawing."

In another ambulance a girl lay bundled on a stretcher.

"Any heartbeat?" an EMT woman snapped.

"Not yet."

"All right, continue chest compressions. I'll intubate her and start suction." The woman used a laryngoscope to insert a tube through the girl's mouth down into her trachea.

"You got foam?" the other EMT asked.

"Sure do. She sucked in a lot of lake water."

"How long do you think she was under?"

"No idea."

"Okay, suction finished. I got out about fifty cc's of fluid. Starting ventilation." The woman began squeezing the ventilator bag that was hooked up to an oxygen tank. The EMT stopped the chess compressions. He pressed a stethoscope to her chest.

"Got a heartbeat! Very weak." The EKG monitor showed a very slow heart rate.

"Call in to the ER and tell them what we're coming in with."

"Hello, this is Pete coming in with a patient, approximately thirteen-year-old girl, found in Lake Marian. She initially needed CPR but responded to chest compressions, suction, and O$_2$. Continuing ventilation, weak pulse with a heart rate of forty-two."

The woman lifted the girl's eyelids and shone the beam of a small penlight into them.

"Any pupil contraction?"

"None."

"No pupil contraction," Pete reported.

Was she dead? thought Brianna. She wasn't sure. But wherever she was, it wasn't bad. No, not at all. She felt oddly rested and free. She wondered what her parents would think. Did they think? Their perfect little girl had fallen from grace, and now right through the ice. Her mom's dream wrecked. The career her mother never had but instead foisted onto her daughter. Was it gone? Brianna smiled slightly in her comatose state. And was her parents' marriage gone too? Her dad had moved out weeks ago. No more International House of Pancakes, no more breakfasts on Sunday where she had to pretend to be happy. International House of Pancakes, refuge for divorced parents granted weekly visitation rights with their children. Children they had hardly known how to speak to in the first place. Done with that. No more. But in the back of Brianna's almost-dying, gasping brain, she had another thought. She could not quite remember what it was, but it was vital. It had meaning. There was something she had done—something important, of value, not to her but to someone else. She had maybe saved a life of someone? What was it? If only she could recall it, then she might leave in peace. Marisol . . . Marisol . . .

"She's a remarkable woman, your grandmother," Dr. Freed said as he tapped the rail at the end of her hospital bed. "The pacemaker is doing the job."

"The marvels of twenty-first-century medicine," Gran said. "To think how it was . . . way back when . . ." *Careful, Gran*, Rose thought. The image of those crazy doctors bleeding Queen Mary was still vivid in her mind. She knew the phantom baby had never shown up.

"I think you can go home tomorrow. And this wonderful granddaughter will be able to get back to school."

Her gran's "slight heart attack," as they referred to it, had happened on a Friday night, and now it was Tuesday. They had told Sam Gold about the ICE men coming to their door. He advised Marisol not to go to school for a few days. He himself planned to go directly to the school and talk with Ms. Fuentes, the principal, about the Mean Queens' call to the immigration authorities.

Just as the doctor was leaving the room, there was the ping of a text message coming through on Rose's phone. It was Joe.

> You won't believe this, but the Trio of Doom might truly be a doomed trio—Carrie, Lisa, and that twerp, the one you call Tinker Bell. But you know who is in deeper trouble? Brianna. She's in a coma at St. Vincent's Hospital!!!! She broke through the ice the same night your grandmother had her heart attack.

"Whoa!!!" Rose blurted out.

Dr. Freed, who was halfway out the door, turned abruptly. "Something wrong, Rose?"

"Uh . . . I just found out that, uh . . ." Should she say friend? Yes, she should. "That a friend of mine is in a coma here at the hospital."

"Oh yes, there was a girl who fell through the ice on Lake Marian. I think it was the same night they brought your grandmother in. She's downstairs in critical care. No visitors except family."

"Yeah, sure."

But Rose decided to go down anyhow. She couldn't stay away.

The intensive care unit rooms all had very large glass walls. There were privacy curtains, but she saw immediately that the one in Brianna's room had not been drawn. There were three people in the room. One was a doctor who stood at the foot of the bed, a stethoscope around his neck. Then there were two others, a man and a woman, beside the bed. Those two must be Brianna's parents. They looked frozen in place. There was a network of tubes all connected to one thing—Brianna, who lay very still on the bed, draped in sheets. Half a dozen screens flickered with incomprehensible numbers on machines that Rose figured must be monitoring her breathing rate, her heart rate, and who knew what else. Her brain waves? Rose closed her eyes and swallowed. *Poor Brianna....*

A doctor came by, trailed by three medical students. "This is a thirteen-year-old girl who fell through the ice while skating. She can't breathe for herself, so she is on a ventilator. We're getting some conflicting information about brain activity. She appears totally unresponsive to any stimulus."

"Consciousness extinct?" a woman student asked.

"Hard to determine at this point. She could very possibly be hearing but unable to respond or signal in any perceivable way."

Inside the room, Rose could see that the doctor was addressing Brianna's parents.

"You know, Mr. and Mrs. Gilbert, it's just very difficult to tell at this point. We'll be doing a stimulus assessment later today. There is a distinct possibility that Brianna can hear us but is not able to respond."

"But if she flunks . . ." Meg Gilbert's voice reached a desperate pitch.

Flunks, Mom! Jeez, Brianna thought.

"Will that mean—what do they call it? A persistent . . . uh, vegetative state?" Meg Gilbert asked.

Oh boo-hoo, Mom, you'll have a vegetable instead of a skater!

Brianna was in a peculiar place. A kind of dream-scape. She could hear her parents but really had no desire to respond. She was skating but perhaps not on ice. Clouds? On the crests of waves? A far and distant sea? She decided to try a double axel. Yes, a double axel. What did she have to lose? Her life? Her brain? The sounds of the machines supporting her life melted into beautiful music. *Is this heaven?* she wondered.

"You're telling me she's not there?!" Sara Morton hissed at the two guards, one of whom held a warrant for the arrest of Rose Ashley.

"Not a trace, miss."

"But I saw her leave her quarters less than ten minutes ago. I saw her shadow slip around the corner. She must be in the laundry now. She was going with some muslin items for the queen's lying-in." Sara was furious. "Come with me. She has to be there."

She stomped off in a rage of indignation. Half a minute later she spied something white on the stone floor. Like a bloodhound on a scent, she bent over and picked it up. "Hah!" she exclaimed, and held up a muslin cloth triumphantly. "Proof! This is a baby diaper! They need to be washed at least twenty times to be soft enough for a baby's bum."

From behind a statue Bettina peeked out and quickly began turning somersaults into their path.

"Out of the way, you cursed little ball of . . . of blubber," Sara screeched. But no sooner had Bettina retreated than Jane pranced out and for the first time in years performed a perfect cartwheel.

"And now you!" Sara shouted.

"Yes, me, Jane the Fool! And cock-a-doodle-doo to you!" She made a huge sweeping bow and then began dancing in circles around them.

"You idiot, you! Follow me to the laundry," Sara yelled to the guards.

Bettina and Jane exchanged nervous glances.

"God speed the child," Jane whispered, taking Bettina's hand and giving it a squeeze.

"Try not to worry," Bettina said. "Rose has a knack for just disappearing."

"That she does. Have never quite understood it. But she does have that knack."

Finally Sara and the two guardsmen arrived at the laundry. Clouds of steam from the huge vats of boiling water hung in the air. A dozen red-faced women stood at scrub boards scouring clothes in basins. Another very hefty woman walked up to the trough into which fresh hot water was poured.

"Out o' the way, lads, unless you want to get boiled like hams."

"Where's Rose?" she demanded.

"Rose?" asked one of the laundresses.

"Yes, Rose the seamstress," Sara barked.

"I could have sworn she was here a minute ago with that fresh pile of diapers to be washed. But she vanished. Just vanished into thin air. Sweet girl," one of the laundresses said, scratching her head.

"Hardly thin air in here," said another. "Thick as fog off Ballyhoo Rock."

Chapter 32

"Someone over There Misses You"

Marisol greeted Rose and her grandmother the next morning. She had a huge smile on her face.

"Welcome, Abuela."

"Abuela!" Gran exclaimed. "Isn't that the loveliest-sounding word for grandmother? Yes, I'm back, and I have a clock inside me."

"It's a pacemaker, Gran. Not really a clock."

"No matter." Gran waved her hand. "It keeps time for my heart. That's how I think of it."

"I'll get Betty to help you upstairs." Then Marisol burst out, "Mr. Gold says my papers might come today!"

"Oh!" Rose and her gran both exclaimed.

"Wonderful. Just wonderful, Marisol. I shall truly be your abuela."

When Rose and Betty got her upstairs and tucked into bed, Rosalinda beckoned her granddaughter to come closer.

"I want to tell you something." Rose bent over. Her gran began to whisper in her ear.

"You know, I think you've spent enough time with me. I do think you should be getting back, dear child."

"Getting back, Gran?"

"You know where. It came upon me in a dream when I was in the hospital. I just have this feeling that someone over there misses you."

"Okay, Gran. But it's daytime."

"What's the difference? Day, night—*whatever*, as you youngsters say!"

"All right," Rose said, and began heading downstairs toward the greenhouse.

"Where are you going?" Marisol asked.

"Uh, just to the greenhouse to check on something. Be right back."

"I'm sure you will," Marisol said with a sly smile.

Rose walked into the greenhouse. She stopped as always by the graftling.

"Lookin' good!" she murmured. She swore it had grown an inch in the last couple of days.

It was June. No baby had yet appeared. But had expectations changed? Not a wit—at least not that Rose could see. Although everyone knew there was little history of a baby ever taking eleven months to be born, everyone was talking of its birth with as much certainty as before. In fact, the court goldsmith was said to have already arrived at Hampton Court. Bettina had told her, "Any minute he'll be consulting with Her Majesty about the birth medals." Rose was trying to figure out how she would explain all this to her father. She had to choose the moment carefully. Then, as she crossed an interior courtyard, she saw two men coming her way. Prince Felipe and—*OMG, Dad!* What could she do?

"Ah, the little seamstress!" the prince called out. She could see the color drain from her father's face. Rose dipped into a deep curtsy. "Ah, my dear, you are a beam of sunshine on this rather dreary day. Now, I have completely forgotten your name . . . ?"

"Rose," she whispered, and saw her dad's lips barely moving around the sound of her name.

"Exactly. Yes, pardon me for not remembering," the prince said. He turned to Nicholas Oliver. "Now, this young lady, good sir—she deserves a medal. She has sewn many of the garments for our expected child. Pehaps a rose medallion. A rose for a rose!"

"Indeed, Your Highness!" Rose could not believe this

conversation. Her father's eyes seemed to ignite with a glittering fury.

"But I believe, Your Highness," Rose began to say, "that it is against the custom of the court for anybody except for a Tudor to wear such a rose—the Tudor Rose."

The prince rolled his eyes. "By the blood of our savior, that is a stupid rule."

"But so it is—a law," Rose's father said, regaining his calm.

"I must be off, Your Highness." She paused. "Sir," she added, nodding to her father. "I have an errand outside the palace. I must go to the apothecary for some herbs Dr. Calagila has ordered to be on hand for the birth." She looked directly at her father as she spoke.

Half an hour later as Rose rounded a wooded corner on the high road to the village, Nicholas Oliver stepped out from behind a great oak. He looked different. He was not wearing his court clothes at all. The embroidered doublet was gone. Instead he wore a simple leather jerkin. Also replaced was the plush velvet bonnet. On his head her father wore a woven wide-brimmed hat to protect him from the sun. He was in the dress of a yeoman farmer.

"Dad! Oh, Dad, are you mad at me?!"

"Never." She ran into his arms. "Come, child, let us walk as a father and daughter should, hand in hand down this road." He paused as if he had just thought of something. "Oh God's toes, I nearly forgot. I have something to show you. Come with me." He walked toward the enormous old oak tree. At the back there was a patch of bare trunk where the bark had fallen or been scraped away.

"So you see it?" he asked. She looked up to where he was pointing. There was a heart, and within the heart were the initials *N.O. + R.A.*

Rose lifted her hand and touched the letters. She felt a tingling run down her spine. "My mom touched this and carved her name."

"Indeed. I know what you're thinking. Tree hugger!"

It surprised Rose that he knew this expression, but her mom was a big environmentalist. She wouldn't have liked the idea of carving anything into a tree.

"But," continued her father, "the bark had already been stripped away. I told her many people declared their love this way. Why not us? And she asked me how old I thought the tree is. I said maybe five hundred years or so. And all of a sudden she said, 'Give me your dagger, Nick.' And she is the one who carved it."

"Why? Why do you suppose she did this?"

Her father waited a long time to reply. "I think she was already feeling she might have to leave for good. I think it was a kind of goodbye to me." His eyes filled with tears. "But look, here you are, saying hello to me."

"So, Dad, you're really not mad at me for coming back?" He shook his head. "Dad, I want you to come back with me to my home in Indiana, and Franny too."

A pained look crossed his face. "Franny is in danger, grave danger. Through my . . . my contacts, I know her name is on a list."

Rose gasped. "No! No!"

"I'm trying to get her out."

"Out to where?"

"But that's not all, Rose. I just found out this afternoon from Jane."

"Jane the Bald?" So Jane was a spy as well! Rose had suspected that.

"Yes, Jane the Fool, who is no fool at all. Jane feels that your name might be on a list as well."

"Mine? Why me?"

"Has the queen asked you to sew any clothes for the baby of late?"

Come to think of it, she hadn't worked on any clothes. Perhaps some muslin diapers, but that was all. Sara had been called back into service as the principal seamstress. And Rose had successfully avoided crossing paths with her. But she had sewn nothing since the gowns with the bunnies.

"She thinks the baby is cursed because you are not a true Catholic."

There was only one person who could have told the queen something like that—Sara!

"It doesn't matter if it's true or not. When she gets an idea in her head, she pays no heed to anything else."

"Sara Morton put that thought in her head."

"Never mind who did it. It's why I came. I wasn't sure you were back. But I had a feeling."

"You must be the only one."

"The only one what?" he asked.

"The only one who knew I had left. No one ever seems to notice. It's as if I leave a shadow behind that just carries on."

"That was the way it was with your mum. But when you truly love someone, as I loved your mother, you begin to sense when she is not here. When you are simply dealing with . . . a specter, a ghost of that person."

"It's all so strange, Dad. In my world, my century, the twenty-first, I could die in a car crash like Mom, or some awful accident." At this moment she thought of Brianna in the intensive care unit, having a machine breathe for her. "Or just die of old age. But here . . . here . . ."

"Here you could die very young, tied to a chair with kindling piled about your legs and set afire with a torch."

"I have to get out."

"And leave no shadows behind. You must get out forever, Rose. Forever!"

"How?"

"I have a plan. There is a ship leaving from Southampton."

"But Southampton is far from here."

"We'll leave tonight. But do not go back to the palace. I'll come on a horse and bring another as soon as it's dark. Meet me at the split in the Blackheath Road. There's a grove of trees on the left side. I'll also bring clothes. Boy's clothes. We'll ride there. It will take two days."

"And Franny?"

"Franny is already there."

"But will I be missed by the palace?"

"No, Jane will cover for you."

"Jane?"

"Jane and Bettina."

"But where are we going?"

"Across the channel to France."

"France!"

"Yes, the court of King Henri, but more important, you will serve the Little Queen."

"Little Queen?"

"Mary, Queen of Scots, the queen without a country."

Chapter 33

Welcome
to America

The light lingered during the long June day. It would not grow dark for another two hours or so. Her father had said he would not come until dark. Rose sat down beneath the oak tree—just under the heart carved by her mother, the tree hugger. Rose giggled a bit when she thought of those two words coming out of her dad's mouth. How strange this all was. But now under the spreading branches of the oak she felt not just safe but happy. But should she feel safe? *Oh, give me this moment, just this moment,* she thought, for it was almost as if both her parents were right there embracing her, wrapping their arms around her in the leafy shade of the tree. She drifted off to sleep—or was it a dream? But someone was struggling—struggling for breath. Then she heard the sound of laughter, celebration—and there was a balloon bouquet. *I want to go back . . . just for a bit.*

And she was back, standing in the greenhouse. The graftling had grown now perhaps three inches and she saw the swell of buds forming on the stem, but from the entry hall there were raucous, joyful sounds. She rushed out of the greenhouse. Susan Gold, her father, and his wife, Eleanor, were all there, and Marisol was holding a bouquet of red, white, and blue balloons.

Susan squealed. "The papers came through! They came through. Your grandmother is officially Marisol's sponsor!"

"And," Sam Gold said, "Marisol has taken her first step toward citizenship."

"And," Susan added, "certain Mean Queens are in deep doo-doo."

Rose rushed toward Marisol and hugged her. She actually lifted her off her feet.

"Now I'll drive you girls to school," Susan's father said.

"Wait a minute," Rose said. She bit her lip lightly. "How is Brianna? If it hadn't been for her . . ."

"We don't know yet," Sam Gold replied. "Her condition is still very precarious."

"I wish there were some way to tell her that Marisol is safe."

"I don't think that's possible," Susan said. "At least not right now."

Twenty minutes later, Rose and Susan, with Susan's father, walked into Ms. Fuentes's office. Mr. Ross was also there, looking very somber.

"And so we meet again!" Ms. Fuentes said, bitterly casting her eyes at the three girls—Carrie, Lisa, and Jenny—who were sitting in chairs against the wall. "I was telling the girls about my experiences coming to this country as a child, an unaccompanied minor. It is unbelievable to me that you three would do what you did. Steal into my office and call Immigration and Customs Enforcement to report Marisol from my telephone. First of all, that is breaking and entering."

"It was all Brianna's idea."

"Brianna's idea!" Rose roared. "That is a total lie. It was Brianna who warned us that you had done this. No! No! NO! You are all liars. And now Brianna might be dying."

Rose felt a hand on her shoulder. It was Mr. Gold. She stopped talking.

He stepped closer to the three girls. "Carrie, Lisa, Jenny, look at me." Reluctantly the girls shifted their gazes from the floor to Samuel Gold's face. It was a long face with a somewhat gray cast. Rose felt as if she had never seen such a stern and serious face. It could have been carved in granite. "Ms. Fuentes and I have discussed appropriate measures to be taken for this behavior."

Punishment, Rose thought. *Why doesn't he say that?*

"We have concluded that every day after school, you must report to immigration court. You will be met there by some of our best lawyers as they represent young minors who have either arrived alone or been separated from a parent at the border. The first case on the docket today is that of Julieta Ariz. She is four years old. She was separated from her older brother at the border." He paused as if to let that sink in. "She is four years old and will walk into a courtroom only accompanied by a lawyer she has just met. That lawyer is Louise Ryan, who will plead her case. Little Julieta is not a criminal. She is a child who came to this country like so many of us, or our parents or great-grandparents or great-great-grandparents. And they saw those words on the metal plaque at the Statue of Liberty:

> *"Give me your tired, your poor,*
> *Your huddled masses yearning to breathe free,*
> *The wretched refuse of your teeming shore.*
> *Send these, the homeless, tempest-tost to me,*
> *I lift my lamp beside the golden door!"*

A quiet descended on the room as Mr. Gold turned to Marisol. "Marisol, welcome to America."

That evening Marisol helped Rose in the greenhouse after they had finished their homework. "We need to thin out those love-lies-bleeding sproutlings."

"What funny names for flowers."

"Old English names, I think," Rose said.

Marisol looked up at her. "Are you going back?" They had not talked about Rose's trips, her time migrations, since that evening when Rose had tried to take Marisol with her.

"I think so. . . . There are still some . . . some unfinished things there. I won't be long."

Marisol leaned across the tray where she was starting to thin out the sprouts. "Can I . . ."

Rose gasped. "You want to come?"

"Oh, no. No, I'm here to stay, but I want to watch you go."

"You do?" Marisol nodded. "Well, I suppose so."

"How do you do it?"

"I'm not really sure how it happens. I sort of . . . well . . . you know . . . concentrate on something." Rose's hand went to her neck, where once for a brief moment in time she had worn the locket her father had made of the Tudor Rose.

Marisol watched, mesmerized, as a vaporous mist began to form around Rose and she slowly dissolved, leaving just a shadow behind. Then a whisper came from the mist. "I'll be back in just a minute or two."

Marisol nodded. "I know," she said softly. "I know, *amiga . . . hasta luego.*"

Chapter 34

Another Mary, Another Queen

*R*ose recalled the swells beneath the ship—*the* Flying Sparrow. She remembered herself and Franny holding hands tightly as they saw the coast of France appearing like a sketchy line on the horizon at dawn. It was a memory she had not forgotten in the least, yet she had not directly experienced it. Her shadow had. Her ghostly counterpart that seemed to carry on without her. Perhaps what she remembered so clearly was the air, the wind—salt air brought on a brisk breeze that had scrubbed away the terrible scent of the burnings. By the time they had sailed out of the harbor of Southampton, over two hundred people had died at the stake. Rose's father had not come. This of course had shocked her. She had assumed he would accompany her. "But someday," he had promised. "Someday." But did someday mean just to France or all the way to her home century and Indiana?

Franny had been in the scullery at Hatfield, but had advanced to become an assistant to the pastry chef on occasion. Mrs. Belson, the cook at Hatfield, had taught her well. By this time Rose and Franny had been in the French court for several months. And finally she had remembered to bring her iPhone! In addition, Rose had the diary she had started when she was at Hampton Court Palace during Queen Mary's interminable pregnancy. She wasn't sure how she happened to have it, but she found it in her pocket on the ship while crossing the Channel, along with her iPhone. A great export-import feat to have both. She hadn't dared use the iPhone yet. But she would.

The queen's baby of course never came. Things were very different here in the French court. There were babies and children all over the palaces. Nine children in all, ranging from toddlers to teenagers. Queen Catherine, wife of King Henri, seemed to pop out a baby every two years or so. She was not much fun, Queen Catherine—a dour, rather squat woman—but her husband was just the opposite. And the Little Queen, Mary Stuart, with her best friends—all named Mary—provided enough gaiety for everyone. Mary Stuart had been sent to France when she was barely five years old. It had shocked Rose when she found out that at that age Mary Stuart had become engaged to the French king and queen's son Francis, the dauphin—an odd word for "heir to the throne" that the French used. The two had become best friends. It was very hard to imagine them as husband and wife, which they now were.

Rose occupied an odd place somewhere between servant and friend. The Little Queen confided often in Rose, more so, Rose felt, than she did with the Marys, her closest friends. The court had recently moved to Chenonceau Palace, a beautiful chateau on the river Cher. Rose loved her tiny room tucked up in a turret overlooking the river that, now glazed with ice, looked like a pale gray satin ribbon.

She was in her room, repairing a small tear in a gown, when there was a knock on the door.

"Come in," Rose called out. The Little Queen entered. She was actually not that little, but instead, like Rose, quite tall for her age. Rose immediately popped up and then sank into a deep curtsy.

"Up! Up! I need to talk to you and you must swear to tell no one of this conversation."

"Yes, Your Majesty."

Mary's face pulled into a tight grimace. "I am a majesty of Scotland, of France, and someday England." There was something in her voice that seemed to suggest a question more than a fact. "You believe this, don't you, Rose?"

"Of course, Your Majesty." The queen suddenly looked quite vulnerable.

"I worry sometimes, you know. I . . . I mean . . . well . . ." She began wringing her hands. There was something she wanted to say but couldn't quite bring herself to. "I mean, I know that Queen Mary Tudor of England is not very pretty."

"Not very."

"And she's old."

"Yes."

"But what about Princess Elizabeth? Is she prettier than me? Now tell the truth. Is she?"

Rose thought a long time before answering. "She's older than you."

"Nine years older," Mary said.

"She's a different kind of pretty. You have a softer look. She looks a bit harsher."

"She's supposed to be very smart."

"Yes, I think she is."

"I think I'm smart, but I'm never sure . . . uh . . . how should I put this?" Rose was uncertain where this conversation was going. She didn't know what to say. Within seconds, tears were streaming from the Little Queen's eyes. "I shouldn't be talking this way." She suddenly grasped Rose's hands. "But Rose, I feel I can say these things to you. You once told me how your mother had died and you weren't sure what had happened to your father. That he is not . . . not around. So you see, I think—well, of course you're not royal—but we do share some things." *Like what?* Rose thought. "I mean. My mother is not dead. But I have not seen her since I was four years old. She is alive somewhere—well, in Scotland. But she might as well be on the moon. But if I become queen, no one can keep me from her ever again!"

It suddenly dawned on Rose that indeed they did share something: an unavailable parent. In Rose's case, a father she was deprived of acknowledging or seeing in this world. And for Mary Stuart, a mother from whom politics had separated her. They were both orphans of sorts.

"I mean, Francis is nice. He's my husband, after all. But it's not the same as having a mother."

Duh! Rose thought. This was precisely why kids her age shouldn't get married. But it was the sixteenth century and sex ed and all that stuff hadn't been invented.

"Uh . . . Your Majesty," Rose began hesitantly.

"Oh, don't call me that."

"Ma'am."

"I suppose that's all right, but here in the privacy of your own room you could call me just Mary."

"Mary, maybe you will become queen of England, and then you can see your mother all you want."

"Exactly. It won't be dangerous then. You see, they have to keep us apart. Politics. Stupid politics." Rose was unsure who "they" were. "But if I become queen, everything will work out. I'm sure." She paused and looked into Rose's eyes. "Aren't you sure, Rose?"

"Uh . . . yes. I'm sure," Rose lied. She lied because she knew the end of the story. But what could she do? Tell her that her head would be cut off? Not right away. Not for another thirty years or so. Small comfort!

They would never speak of it again, but a week later, on a very cold winter evening, Rose was once more in her room, having just finished a new gown for the Christmas holidays, specifically for St. Stephen's Day, which was the merriest of the twelve days of Christmas in the court. She took out her diary, just rolled-up pieces of paper. Too bad they didn't have staplers here, she thought. Her first diary entry in France was from eight months before.

Dear Diary,

I was right when I told Princess Elizabeth that white could become very popular in the future for weddings. When Mary, Queen of Scots, married Francis yesterday, she wore a pure white gown. Well, actually sort of white on white, or cream on white. It caused great controversy, as white is considered the color of mourning here in France. I worked on the dress along with six other seamstresses. She was married at the Cathedral of Notre-Dame in Paris. Now, here is the interesting part. During the many days of the wedding festivities, the court stayed in the palace of the Louvre, and it was there that I met a very strange man—a favorite of Queen Catherine. His name is Nostradamus. He is an astrologer, or some call him a seer, as it is said that he can look into the future. He often gives his predictions in short puzzling rhymes. On the day the dress was finished, he came up to me when I was least expecting it and stood right in front of me. He began to speak to me, but it was as if he were in a trance of some sort. Here is exactly what he said:

"You saw the white in a distant light.
The bride does not mourn, but some do scorn.
A new life begins,
a new fashion wins."

I was shocked. I didn't know what to say. Does this seer know my secret—my secret double life? For that is how I now think of my strange experience. It is as if I am living two lives in the space of one.

Rose closed the diary. There was a soft knock on her door.

"Who's there?"

"C'est moi, chère Rose." It was Princess Claude of France, the seventh-born of Queen Catherine and King Henri's children. She was a delightful girl of about eleven years old. The same age as Princess Elizabeth had been when Rose first arrived at Hatfield.

"What can I do for you, Princess Claude?"

"The queen wants you to come out and skate with us. The ice is perfect."

"Which queen?" Rose asked, and smiled.

Princess Claude giggled. "Not the *reine mère*."

"Ah, your *belle-soeur*." Rose's French had improved greatly. *Belle-soeur* was the word for "sister-in-law."

"*Oui*, Rose, Mary the Queen of Scots." Then a mischievous look gleamed in her eyes. "*Maman est trop grosse pour patiner.*"

"Your mother is too fat to skate, but she dances beautifully." Catherine de Medici was an exquisite dancer.

"*C'est vrai,*" Princess Claude said.

"All right. I'll come down in a few minutes."

"*Merci!*" Princess Claude said gleefully, and skipped out the door.

Rose could not help thinking how different life was here from that of the royal court in England. Perhaps it was that there were so many children, and she and Franny were often called upon to join in their games and amusements. And ice skating was one of the favorite games here at Chenonceau. The cold had come early this year, and the river had frozen solid by mid-November.

Rose bundled herself in her warmest cloak and put on extra stockings in addition to a muffler made of fur. The fur of a white fox. It had been a cast off by one of the many little princesses. On her head she wore what was called a patch hat. Such a hat was patched together from the fur of at least four different animals. No one in this century had ever heard of animal cruelty or organizations like PETA— People for the Ethical Treatment of Animals. *I am a PETA nightmare*, Rose realized as she waddled out of her small bedroom swathed in fur. But hey, parkas had not been invented yet. The last thing she wanted to do was freeze her butt off.

The ice was perfect. There were at least two dozen people, children and adults, gliding across the glistening surface of the river. There was lots of laughter and talking and even music. Yes, some of the court's favorite musicians were bundled up and playing lutes and violins at the edge of the ice on this starry night. Mary Stuart was skating arm in arm with Francis. She was, in fact, practically holding him up. At least a head taller than the frail little dauphin and almost two years older, she was definitely the athlete in the couple, Rose thought. Francis was not yet fifteen and Mary was sixteen. It was ridiculous that they were even married, in Rose's mind. What was even more ridiculous was that originally they were supposed to have been married when Francis was eleven and Mary Stuart was thirteen!

The scene on the frozen river before her now made Rose think of that evening on Lake Marian, the bonfire, the sight of Brianna skimming across the ice—sealed in a kind of unfathomable loneliness. She could not help but wonder if Brianna was still alive. The terrifying image of her in the intensive care unit hooked up to those machines and monitors began to haunt Rose. Was Brianna still breathing? Was her heart still beating? It was almost as if she could hear the gasping sounds, or was it the pumping of the ventilator that was breathing for Brianna? Suddenly she noticed a hush had fallen over the frozen river. And then there was a collective gasp as people caught sight of a figure who seemed to have emerged from nowhere.

Brianna!

The figure leaped into the air, twirled about, then landed. Everyone else had stopped skating. They watched mesmerized as the girl skated backward at great speed. She did spins and spirals and waltzing steps and toe loop jumps.

"What's that she just did?" little Princess Claude came up to Rose and whispered.

"A lutz, I think they call it. When you take off from one skate, then twirl up into the air and land on the opposite skate. . . ."

"But who is she?"

"Oh . . ." Rose did not know what to say.

"Who is she, Rose?" Princess Claude tugged on her hand.

"Her name is Brianna and she comes from far, far away." *In time and place*, Rose thought. But was she alive, or was she a ghost from Rose's other life? Rose didn't know, but suddenly the skater dissolved into the night.

"Where did she go?" someone asked.

"Where did she come from?" asked another.

A week had passed since the mysterious events on the frozen river.

"I really like this one, Francis. What do you think for a spring ball gown?" Mary asked the dauphin.

"Everything becomes you, my dear." Francis looked toward his father, King Henri, as if to confirm that he had said the right thing.

Rose always nearly giggled when Francis, who was the size of a fifth grader, called his wife "my dear." It was as if they were both playacting at being married. Rose was in the presence chamber of Mary, Queen of Scots, showing her some new fabrics that had arrived from the silk weavers in Tours. A guard entered.

"Your Majesty," he said, addressing King Henri. "An envoy from England has arrived with an urgent message." The king's and Mary's faces brightened as if they were anticipating something wonderful. The air seemed to shiver.

Rose had to clap her hand over her mouth to stifle a yelp as her father entered the room.

Nicholas Oliver made a deep bow and avoided even glancing at Rose.

"Your Majesty, I bear news. Queen Mary Tudor of

England has died. The princess . . ." There was a sharp inhalation of breath at the word "princess." It was as if the entire room had gasped and all the air had been sucked out. "Elizabeth is declared queen. God save Queen Elizabeth!" A silence as heavy as lead descended on the room.

King Henri looked stricken. Mary, Queen of Scots, collapsed in a faint. "Smelling salts!" someone cried out. Her husband, little Francis, turned white and covered his mouth as if he were about to vomit—which he did a few seconds later, on the fabric for the spring ball gown.

A servant appeared and knelt by the collapsed Little Queen. She opened her eyes. *"Vous voulez dire que je ne suis pas reine d'Angleterre."* Rose's French was good enough to understand: *You mean I am not queen of England?* She looked toward Rose as if somehow Rose could solve this probem.

"This is not finished!" King Henri's voice cut the air like a scythe. *"Non, jamais.* Never. My daughter-in-law is queen of England and my son Francis is king."

Within a short time a queen had died, a father had returned to his daughter, and a king was about to start trouble.

A whole mess of trouble, Rose thought. And then an expression that her mom had sometimes used streamed through Rose's mind. *Time to get out of Dodge!*

Epilogue

A favorable wind carried Rose, her father, and Franny across the Channel. It was bitterly cold. Franny and Rose were leaning against the shrouds near the foremast. "You dragged us up here from below for what, Rose Ashley?"

"A selfie."

"What in the world is a selfie?"

"A picture of ourselves." Rose took her iPhone out from a pocket.

Franny gasped. "Oh . . . I mean, OMG. This is one of those OMG moments, isn't it?"

"Yes it is, Franny."

"You're going to make a photogone of us. Like the ones in the locket."

"Photograph. Not photogone. Kind of the reverse. You won't be gone from me." Rose's voice dropped.

"You mean when you go away. So you are going?"

"Uh . . . it depends."

"On your father, right?"

Rose nodded. She looked toward the stern of the ship, where her father stood, looking down at the wake. She wouldn't take a picture of him. He wasn't going to be gone. She'd bring him back with her. If not this time . . . sometime in these tangles of time. She would, she swore.

Nicholas Oliver looked at the wake curling out from the stern of the ship. *My daughter won't give up*, he thought. She was too much like her mum. Her mum hadn't given up trying to get him to go back until . . . until her life was taken. He felt his eyes filling with tears. *Am I crazy not to go? . . . But what would I do there?* He felt an arm thread through his as he leaned against the rail.

"Love your daughter." He looked shocked. He must have spoken these words out loud.

Nicholas put his arm around her shoulders and they turned to watch as the coastline of England came into sight, just a scratchy line at first, but as they watched, gradually the green hills melted out of the mist. "So green!" Rose exclaimed.

"Indeed," her father said. He began to speak in a low, musical voice.

This royal throne of kings, this sceptred isle,
This earth of majesty, this seat of Mars,
This other Eden, demi-paradise,
This fortress built by Nature for herself
Against infection and the hand of war,
This happy breed of men, this little world,
This precious stone set in the silver sea,
Which serves it in the office of a wall
Or as a moat defensive to a house,
Against the envy of less happier lands,
This blessed plot, this earth, this realm, this England.

Rose was mesmerized by the words. "Dad, what is that?"

"Shakespeare, *King Richard II*, act two, scene one."

"But Dad, Shakespeare hasn't been born yet."

"Right you are! Not for another six years—1564, to be exact."

"So how did you know this?"

"Your mum, of course."

"Mom!"

"She was an English literature major. University of Michigan. Graduated with honors."

Rose's face broke into a huge smile. "See, Dad, I told you you'd catch up. You're at least six years ahead of yourself!"

And then within two more days they were back at Hatfield. Together she, Franny, and her father walked up the winding road to the redbrick palace.

"Ah, welcome back!" Mrs. Dobkins, the head housekeeper, greeted them in the kitchen entryway. "And Franny, Cook has missed you so much. I think now you are officially out of the scullery and into the pastry department. And you, my dear, well, you must go directly to the queen. She wants to discuss her coronation gown."

Rose went upstairs. Once more she walked through the presence chamber. Not much had changed. An usher told her to go right through to meet with the queen in her private chamber. There were three or four councillors standing near the queen.

One councillor with a trim black beard flecked with gray was speaking. "Your Majesty, now that the Church of England has been restored, in terms of the practicing Catholics would you not consider making them now practice Protestantism?"

"No! There shall be no persecution of any man or woman for their beliefs. I would not open windows into men's souls."

She turned around abruptly. "Ah, my little seamstress is back. Just in time for my coronation."

Rose lowered herself into a deep curtsy. When she lifted herself up again, she saw the locket glowing at Elizabeth's throat. *She might be a queen,* thought Rose, *but she's a thief as well. My locket! Mine!*

31901065390140